Dialogue With a Dead Man

Carter sat with his mouth next to the dying man's ear.

"Yuri. Yuri. It is your last moment. Time to confess," he said in Russian.

The bloodied mouth tried to move but nothing came out.

Carter moved closer. He strained to hear if the breath that was expelled was a last confession.

"Hunger . . ."

"Say it one more time," Carter urged.

"Hung . . . ary . . ."

Carter felt for a pulse again and found none.

NICK CARTER IS IT!

FROM THE NICK CARTER
KILLMASTER SERIES

SANCTION TO SLAUGHTER

KILL MASTER
NICK CARTER

JOVE BOOKS, NEW YORK

Dedicated to the men and women of the
Secret Services of the
United States of America

KILLMASTER #250: SANCTION TO SLAUGHTER

A Jove Book / published by arrangement with
The Condé Nast Publications, Inc.

PRINTING HISTORY
Jove edition / June 1989

ISBN: 0-515-10034-X

Jove Books are published by The Berkley Publishing Group,
200 Madison Avenue, New York, New York 10016.
The name "JOVE" and the "J" logo
are trademarks belonging to Jove Publications, Inc.

PRINTED IN THE UNITED STATES OF AMERICA

10 9 8 7 6 5 4 3 2 1

ONE

The house was set back from Sussex Drive, surrounded by Governor's Bay to the north, Rockliffe Park
to the east, and Rideau Falls to the west. Royal Canadian
Mounted Police officers in plainclothes sat in unmarked
cars opposite the mansion. Special Security Service men
patrolled the grounds and manned the security center
inside. Police boats patrolled Governor's Bay, a bulge in
the Ottawa River not far from the Parliament Buildings.
The focus of their attention was number 24, the house of
the prime minister.

The need for security had doubled since the premier of
Québec arrived the day before. With the separation issue
heating up before Québec voters who would decide for
or against in two weeks, strong feeling ran like super-
heated lava through the capital. The French-speaking
separatist sympathizers had flocked to Ottawa with their
leader. The rest of the province's population, including
people who had immigrated to Québec from almost
every country in the world, opposed the breaking up of
their constitution. To them, it was unacceptable for one

1

of the most liberal of all democracies to be ripped apart and crippled financially by a minority clinging to old traditions.

Jacques Carreau, a stocky middle-aged man of medium height, climbed from the bath in his suite on the second floor and was helped to dress by his man, Arthur. While he was slipping into a light cardigan, Marie Carreau came in without knocking.

"Having him in the house makes me nervous, Jacques," she started without preliminaries. "Living in a fishbowl is bad enough, but this . . ."

Carreau sighed. She was like a continuous tape, always the same message. Marie was a beautiful woman. He had always liked the way her black hair and dark eyes contrasted with her alabaster skin. She was the mother of his son and he still loved her, but she had become shrewish lately. The spotlight had never pleased her. Her attitude had grown worse week by week. Every function, every visitor, had disturbed her.

"Gilles Parisant is an old friend. He will always be welcome in our house," he said, trying to keep his voice calm.

"But he's not the same man we knew," she protested. "When we used to sit around the cafés with him in the old days. . . . I loved him then as you did, you know that," she added, frowning. "But . . . I just don't know . . . he's not the crazy radical who laughed and argued politics with us." She sat, her face taking on a wistful look. But just for a moment. "Back then, we all talked about a better government—a better world." Her features hardened. "Now the two-faced bastard's lying to us half the time." She walked to the window and looked out at the grounds. "Looking back, I think he had his own world in mind all the time, his own selfish, separate world."

A prude when it came to language, he shook his head as much at her logic as her vocabulary. "You're being unreasonable, my dear. We have to keep an open mind."

"Dammit!" she snapped, her face flushed. "He'll go his own way and make you a failure—the prime minister who let it all slip away."

"You know I hate that kind of language, Marie," he said, finally voicing his displeasure.

When his man had slipped out tactfully, she closed the door after him. "You didn't hate it when we were younger, when it was part of our lovemaking," she said, putting her arms around his neck.

"That was long ago, Marie," he replied, disengaging himself. "You haven't grown with our position. I wish—"

"Damn you, Jacques Carreau!" she cried. "I hate all this . . . this damned formality. I hate your treating Parisant with kid gloves. Tell the bastard to shape up or you'll kick his butt."

"Marie, Marie . . . I've explained it to you," he said, throwing up his hands. "I've got to go down to him now. Try to be civil."

"Go down to the traitorous bastard! Go down to the back-stabber!" she yelled as he opened the bedroom door. "If I was a man I'd kill him!"

Carreau's shoulders slumped visibly as he left her to join his guest in the library for a final talk, a last chance to change the man's hard line.

"Mother on the warpath again, Dad?" a youthful voice

asked from behind him. Jules Carreau had opened a door down the hall from his father's room and now followed him along the hall. He was taller than his father, a handsome young man with his mother's dark hair and eyes. At eighteen, he was the heartthrob of Ottawa's teenage girls.

"Don't pay any attention to her, son. She's angry at Gilles."

"Enough to use the word *kill*?"

"You know your mother. She sounds off like that sometimes, but it's all talk."

"I can't blame her," Jules said, his face taking on a brooding look. "Most of my friends feel the same way. The man's going to take away our future. That's what my friends say."

Carreau thought back to what he felt at eighteen. In fact, one of his friends who had agreed with him on revolutionary change was Gilles Parisant. They had spouted their radical philosophies over glasses of beer in Montreal cafés until they were kicked out for disturbing the peace. He had gone on to practice law, to teach law and political science at Montreal University, while Gilles had followed a newspaper career.

Still in his teens, Jules was at the starting gate, the issues all black and white. In a way, Parisant was still like that. While the rest of their friends had tempered their thinking, realizing that nationalism was the only sane economic and social route for Canada, Parisant had been a maverick. To him, everything was still black and white. To the leader of the Parti Québecois, nothing was gray, nothing could be compromised. It had to be all or nothing.

• • •

The next morning the prime minister pulled a comb through his salt-and-pepper hair, covering a bald spot with long strands his barber skillfully left intact, and ran the comb through his still-black beard. Arthur helped him into a gray pin-striped suit and a dark blue Burberry raincoat. He was hatless, as was his custom. He hadn't slept well after the session with Parisant, and his prematurely lined face reflected his tiredness.

As the prime minister descended the long, winding staircase to the first floor of his official residence, Parisant was standing near the door with an aide. The premier of Quebec, a short, thin man with the inevitable cigarette in his mouth, seemed impatient to get the ceremony over with and get home. Every day took him closer to the moment of truth. It was the first day of May. On the fifteenth, the people of Québec would go to the polls and make their choice. He'd either be the leader-hero of a separate state, or just another unsuccessful separatist.

"Let's get it over with," the small man said, his irritation obvious. "I don't know why the hell I agreed to this in the first place."

"You could be gracious just this once, Gilles," Carreau said. "Laying a wreath at the War Memorial is just as symbolic for you as for me. The men who died were from all over the country, including our own province."

"*Our* province? You have a hell of a nerve calling yourself a Québecois."

Their conversation was interrupted while the secret service assigned the two leaders to a car in the middle of a convoy drawn up outside. The day had cleared. The raincoat wouldn't be necessary. Carreau took it off and put it on the seat beside him.

The air smelled of tulips. Thousands, in a multitude of colors, were in full bloom on the grounds of his house this time of year as they were in thousands of flower beds around the capital. The bulbs had been a gift from grateful Dutchmen who never forgot that it was the Canadian government that had harbored their royal family and Canadian forces who had fought their way through the Netherlands to free them from Hitler's tyranny.

As their five-car convoy of armored Cadillacs prepared to pull away, four of them filled with Special Security Service agents, they were led by RCMP officers on motorcycles. Carreau noted that Jules's black van pulled out ahead of them and took off to the east. He smiled to himself as he thought of the freedom of youth. He almost, but not quite, wished he could return to that freedom once again, that he could give Marie the freedom she needed so desperately, the freedom from public scrutiny. He knew now, too late, that he could not change and she would never adjust.

Crowds had formed outside the gates of 24 Sussex Drive. Carreau noted that they were not all cheering. Some raised angry fists. Some of the gestures were for him; some were for the small man sitting beside him.

"The people recognize our differences all too well," Parisant said, blowing a cloud of smoke into the already smoke-filled interior.

Carreau coughed and waved the smoke away. "You were like a rock last night. It was our last time to be reasonable, to discuss the issues," he said, "and you barely listened."

"It was the same old story."

"It was the plain truth. Why the hell can't you see it?" he said, swearing for probably the second or third time since he'd entered politics.

"I've heard all of it so many times before. *Québec can't stand alone*," he parroted. *"We'll be in economic trouble within a year. All the big multinationals will move their headquarters*. It's all horseshit."

"You're all alike, you and all the fools who have been hanging on to your coattails in Québec."

"That's enough, Jacques! I should never have come," Parisant said, raising his voice. "Stupid to come. Stupid."

As they drove along Sussex Drive to the west, they passed over the two bridges of Green Island, the site of Ottawa's city hall. The crowds were thicker near the bridges. It was impossible to see the Rideau Canal or even the water of Governor's Bay.

Now, as they neared the end of Sussex Drive, both men were silent, each with his own thoughts. The convoy angled over to Mackenzie Avenue, past the basilica of Notre Dame Cathedral on the left and toward the Château Laurier Hotel on the right.

They were very close to the cenotaph now. The crowds were four and five deep along the road. At the memorial itself, thousands would await them. With feelings so high, Carreau wondered for the first time if this weekend had been a mistake.

No. He'd had to have this last try at Parisant. They'd sat up until two in the morning going over the issues. It had not changed anything, but at least Carreau knew he'd done all he could.

"This was a stupid idea," Parisant said again, as if echoing his thoughts.

"You might be right. But it's too late to stop now."

"Let's get it over with fast," Parisant said, his voice dull, as if the weight of the world was upon him. "I've got work piled up at home."

The cavalcade stopped. Special Security Service men surrounded the car and opened the door only after checking the crowd.

Carreau stepped out first to a tumultuous ovation. An undertone of opposition rumbled like an orchestra's bass section beneath the cheers.

Parisant slipped out and stood beside Carreau, his head barely coming to the prime minister's shoulder. They were almost hidden by the security agents who formed a human wall around them.

Wreaths had already been placed by others at the base of the monument. A huge new wreath of red roses and green ferns stood on a stand to one side.

The official party walked slowly toward the monument.

"Come on. This is the last stupid, meaningless act I'll perform for your nationalistic society. Make it fast," Parisant mumbled to his old friend.

The area around the base for thirty feet or so had been kept clear. The guards held the crowds back as the two leaders stepped out and walked slowly to the wreath.

Parisant had done this hundreds of times before in countless towns around the country. He lifted the wreath, carried it to the base of the monument, and placed it carefully on a frame left there for the purpose. He looked up at the soldiers cast in bronze for a moment and turned.

Carreau stood looking at him, the sun shining through his sparse hair, its rays glinting from his bald spot.

Parisant reached his side. He started to turn to whisper something to Carreau, when something happened to his face. It began to disintegrate before the prime minister's eyes.

Carreau reached out for his friend as another missile struck the small man in the neck. It spun him around, into Carreau's arms, taking them both off-balance, hurling them to the ground.

Special Security Service men moved quickly to fall over the two leaders and form a human shield above them. Others stood with Uzi machine pistols in their hands, surveying the crowd.

The prime minister had heard no shots. The last thing he remembered was blood pouring from his old friend's shattered throat across his face and off his chin. It smelled like sheared copper and felt like hot syrup. Slowly, the river of his friend's life stopped running. The weight of the bodies on him was too much. A black vortex sucked him down and all was still.

Carreau opened his eyes and looked around. He was in his own bed. Dr. Morrison held one of his wrists. Marie stood at the foot of the bed.

"How do you feel?" Morrison asked.

The scene at the memorial rushed back to envelop him: the smells and sounds that clawed at him; the hot blood that ran off his chin. He turned to reach for a tissue and wretched up some green bile.

"Is Gilles dead?" he asked, his face pale.

"Yes," Morrison replied. He was chief of medicine at Carlton University and official doctor to the cabinet. "James Turner is waiting outside to talk with you. Filbert Hume is on his way from a meeting in Calgary."

Carreau's mind whirled. Turner was the head of the RCMP. He didn't like the man; something about him put the prime minister off. Filbert Hume headed the Special Security Service. The SSS had been formed, early in Carreau's first term, to take over the most sensitive areas of RCMP work. That had been six years ago, and Turner and Carreau had been enemies ever since. The friction was below the surface, out of plain sight, but it was there.

"Show him in," Carreau said. "I want to see him alone."

"I don't think—" Morrison started.

"No buts," Carreau cut in. "I want to see him alone." Dr. Morrison and Marie glanced at each other, then turned and left the room.

Turner entered and towered over the bed. Carreau got out of bed, reached for the robe Arthur had left on a nearby chair, and pulled it on. He gestured for Turner to sit while he paced the room.

"Okay. Now, tell me—how the hell could something like this happen?" he asked. *"How the hell could it happen?"*

"I don't know," Turner said. He was a very big man, at least six-feet-three, and his bulk looked awkward in the antique chair. "We have learned something, however, and it's very bad. Worse than you could imagine . . . something that could ruin you."

"What could be worse?" Carreau exploded.

"We couldn't find the assassin at the memorial. But we found your son Jules in his van with the murder weapon."

Carreau stood stock-still, waiting for Turner to continue.

"He was spaced out on drugs, pulled over to the side of Mountain Road in Gatineau Park about thirty miles north of here."

Carreau slumped in a chair, oblivious of the big man opposite him. Gradually the enormity of the situation dawned on him. It was a setup, but probably a very solid one. Whoever was behind it had probably been planning it for a long time.

But who was responsible? He didn't trust Turner to handle the investigation. He didn't even trust Hume.

"Leave me alone," he said.

"But we have to—"

"Leave me alone!" he shouted.

When Turner had closed the door behind him, Carreau walked to a small office adjoining his bedroom. Several telephones in various colors filled one side of the desk. With tears sliding down his cheeks, he picked up a scarlet one and waited for an answer.

"Let me talk to the president," he said.

TWO

Nick Carter reached for his custom-blended cigarettes on the night table, lit one with his gold Dunhill, and blew smoke to the ceiling. Carol Yao lay beside him, her breathing even, small beads of sweat slowly drying on her pale skin. She was a beautiful woman, tall for a Chinese, her hair black, her eyes a warm brown, her body athletic. She had spent a two-week refresher at the AXE training facility in Virginia not far from Washington. As the new head of the Hong Kong station, she had been called in by Smitty, their chief of Operations, to pick up on all the new data compiled since her last refresher.

Carter was relishing the memory of their lovemaking, when the phone rang. Carol uncoiled like a startled cobra and was immediately alert.

"Yes?" Carter answered on the second ring.

"Hawk wants to see you," a female voice said without preliminaries. It was Ginger Bateman, Hawk's right hand and invaluable assistant.

"Urgent?" he said.

"Urgent enough to pack Carol off to her hotel. Tell her to go straight to her hotel, do not pass GO, do not collect two hundred dollars; she's already had the brass ring."

"Very funny. I'll be about an hour," he said, hanging up.

"Ginger?" Carol asked.

"Correct."

"And she knew I was here?"

"Right again."

"Damn! I swear that woman made a point of finding out if I came here."

He put out his cigarette and rolled toward her, taking her in his arms. "Just a little game she plays. No harm, really."

"I don't like it," she said, putting her arms around his neck and crushing her breasts against his chest. "No such thing as privacy in this game."

"Coming from a culturally inquisitive Chinese lady from Hong Kong, that's a joke," he said with a laugh.

"I'll teach you to laugh," she said, swinging on top of him.

"Teach me well," he chuckled as she straddled his thighs, her hands on his shoulders. "I'll tell them that the traffic was bad," he added. "But this will have to be a short lesson."

While the tulips bloomed in Ottawa, the cherry trees that were almost a national treasure in Washington were not yet in full bloom. Carter wheeled his restored Jaguar XKE from his Georgetown brownstone across the P Street bridge to Dupont Circle. One of the buildings on the circle was the home of Amalgamated Press and Wire

Services, the front for AXE, a supersecret organization formed years earlier by David Hawk at the suggestion of the president. AXE handled covert operations too sensitive for any of the services controlled by the Director of Central Intelligence. The DCI knew of the group's existence, and he sometimes authorized cooperation between the CIA and AXE, but he had learned long ago not to dig too deeply into Hawk's operation or step on any toes. AXE was to remain anonymous to the rest of the intelligence community.

Carter parked the racing-green Jaguar on Church Street. With the fluid motions of a jungle cat, he climbed from the low-slung vehicle and walked to the Amalgamated Press and Wire Services offices. A number of young female heads turned to watch the handsome dark-haired man pass toward the back of the main floor. He palmed the sensor at the elevator and when it recognized his print, he entered and rode it, express, to the inner sanctum.

Ginger Bateman was about to wave him in but he stopped, obviously wanting something from her.

"You're late," she said with a tight smile. "I won't ask for your excuse."

"And you won't get one. What's the mood this morning?"

"He seems concerned. He didn't confide in me."

"What's your guess?"

"I don't guess. Something is going on in Canada."

Carter knocked and when he heard the familiar grunt, he pushed open the door. Hawk stood looking out on the traffic below. With the light framing him, his full head of white hair looked very bright.

Carter had worked with the crusty older man from the beginning. He was Hawk's prize agent, the Killmaster, coded N3: designated to kill in the service of his country.

"You called, sir?" Carter said, standing in an almost military manner.

"Yes, Nick. Sit down," Hawk said, waving him to a chair.

A cigar, its ash an inch long, was clamped between browned teeth, its smoke curling to the ceiling. If Hawk were to retire, Carter mused, it would take a crew of painters a week to get rid of the smell of cigar smoke from the whole upper floor.

"Our president and Prime Minister Carreau are good friends," Hawk said, seating himself behind the desk and blowing another cloud of smoke to the ceiling.

"Common knowledge."

"You didn't listen to the news yesterday or this morning?"

"No," Carter admitted somewhat guiltily. "Something in Canada?"

"Someone put two bullets in the premier of Québec while he was placing a wreath at the War Memorial in Ottawa yesterday morning."

"Parisant is dead? Isn't the referendum just a few weeks away?"

"Thirteen days. The leader of the Parti Québecois was assassinated in Ottawa two weeks before the issue was to be settled."

Carter took a deep breath. He picked one of his monogrammed cigarettes from a gold case and added his own smoke to the blue haze of the room. "A setup to make sure the vote would go their way?" he ventured.

"The separatists have the most to gain," Hawk said. "But in the process they lose a figurehead they can't replace."

"Maybe someone thinks he can fill Parisant's shoes."

"Guy Lafontaine, the deputy premier, will succeed him. He's got to be suspect," Hawk said. "But they think they've got the killer in custody."

"A sacrificial lamb?" Carter asked.

"No. It's Jules Carreau."

"Carreau? A relative of the prime minister?"

"His son."

Carter was silent for a moment, drawing deeply on his cigarette. He let the smoke out slowly and sighed. "Why us?"

"Jacques Carreau doesn't trust James Turner."

"But he's been head of the RCMP for years."

"But he's not Carreau's man. And his hands are dirty, or Carreau has tried to prove they are."

"What about that relatively new division, the Special Security Service?" Carter asked.

"Carreau managed to get a bill through Parliament for the SSS when the RCMP were under investigation. Something like our CIA scandals."

"So why not have their SSS handle the ball?"

"There was a lot of controversy when the bill was passed. It gave them almost unlimited power of search and seizure. No need to show probable cause."

"And they've abused it already?" Carter asked.

"There's a case pending right now," Hawk said, lighting the butt of his cigar that had fizzled out. "It seems they seized seven Sikhs in Vancouver on suspicion of murdering a visiting Indian VIP. The seven turned out to be completely innocent. The SSS violated their rights under their new constitution."

"But it was not enough to discredit the whole SSS."

"It's getting close. Under someone called Filbert Hume, they've acted like fascists. There are too many arrests that look like political manipulation and not enough against organized crime. The press are on their backs and the public's in an uproar."

"Who guarded Carreau and Parisant?" Carter asked. "I presume they were together?"

"The SSS had the job, but the RCMP had some periphery duty."

"So they both blew it."

Hawk was up and pacing as he often did. "Filbert Hume was a political appointment. It seems the Canadians are as stupid about that as we are. When we appoint a new DCI and he's not effective, we at least have deputies in place who can handle the job. With a new service, they didn't have established deputies. So they were in trouble from the start."

"What's my cover?" Carter asked. "I'm sure you've got something devious planned."

"You'll be a U.S. Navy commander. Nicholas Carlson. It's all set up with the Navy people and Thomas Niles, our ambassador to Canada. Sound familiar?"

"If it works . . ."

"Military attaché to the CAF, the Canadian Armed Forces. You'll be assigned officially in three weeks and you're looking over the territory."

"You're right. The cover does sound familiar. Thailand, wasn't it?" Carter said, remembering the case well. "We don't have much time on this one . . ."

"Before the referendum . . . thirteen days."

"I'm working out of the embassy, of course."

"Right across the street from the Parliament Buildings, not a hundred yards from the assassination site."

"Who knows about me at the embassy?"

"Only the ambassador, Niles, a good man. He knows how to keep his mouth shut," Hawk said. "You're unofficially G-2, military intelligence. They've got one of theirs on staff, a woman, Lieutenant Commander Sprague." He consulted a file on his desk. "Her name's Jean. She's been briefed, thinks you're G-2."

"What about the CIA?" Carter asked.

"Keep clear of them. Sprague has her own communications," Hawk said, rolling the cigar to the other side of his mouth.

"Sounds like my kind of assignment," Carter said. "Keep clear of the RCMP, the SSS, and the CIA. But be sure to save poor Jules Carreau from a fate worse than death."

"Get out of here," Hawk said, coming as close to a laugh as he ever managed.

The F-15 pilot dropped an urgent parcel off at the Plattsburg air base, topped up his tanks, and flew on to the Canadian base at Rockliffe. Lieutenant Commander Sprague's car was pulled up on the tarmac. Under his flight suit, Carter had his full dress whites on, a concession to a meeting with the ambassador if that was laid on. As a visitor, he'd be in street clothes most of the time.

Commander Sprague hopped from the nondescript staff car, saluted smartly, and introduced herself. Carter returned the salute, slid in the passenger side, and eyed his driver. She was a blonde with eyes like clear ice. Her uniform was cut severely, but as an expert he knew that the body underneath was well proportioned and athletic. Jean Sprague attempted to hide what nature had so generously given her. Apparently, she scorned makeup or anything that would reveal what she really was, a beauty.

Carter liked what he saw. She appeared to be a no-nonsense woman and Carter figured he'd need that in the brief time frame he'd been given.

She drove out of the airport and got on the road toward Ottawa. "You'll be staying at the Château Laurier. You've got a suite there—all diplomatic treatment. It's Old World, but very central. You'll be able to walk from the embassy."

Carter nodded, and figured now was as good a time as any to pump Jean Sprague. "What should I know before I plunge into this mess up here? I need a crash course."

She took her eyes from the road for a second to look at him, then concentrated once more on the traffic. "Have you ever heard of Robert Boisvert?"

The name didn't ring any bells. "No. Who is he?"

"Minister of foreign affairs and deputy prime minister," she replied.

"He's right up there. What about him?"

"He's sleeping with Marie Carreau, the prime minister's wife."

Carter turned toward Jean. "Is it common knowledge?" he asked intrigued.

"Not that I know of."

"What about Turner and Hume? Their people keep

tabs on the PM's wife, don't they? Don't they provide security?"

"Boisvert and Marie Carreau are thrown together often. Jacques Carreau is a people person. He's away a lot, travels all over the country."

"I thought the prime minister had to attend sessions of Parliament," Carter said.

"The prime minister—or his deputy," Jean informed him.

Carter thought about this for a moment, then asked, "What about the separatists? Do you know Guy Lafontaine?"

Jean nodded. "I've been to Québec City several times and he's here in Ottawa surprisingly often."

"How do you assess him?" Carter asked, lighting a cigarette.

"Ruthless. Boisvert is ambitious, and I think he sleeps with Marie Carreau for pillow talk, but Lafontaine is worse. If you want my gut feeling, I wouldn't put it past him to have had Gilles Parisant killed so he could take over. He's more militant than Parisant could ever have been."

This was a real rogues' gallery, Carter thought. "Tell me about Turner."

"A career policeman. Came up through the ranks. He had no use for politicians who don't understand his job fully."

"How did he and the RCMP get into trouble?"

"Turner ran the department like the last days of Hoover. He was too autocratic and stepped over the line too often. Carreau pared him down to size."

"There must have been bad blood when Carreau set up the SSS and appointed Filbert Hume to head it."

Jean gave a harsh laugh. "That's putting it mildly. Turner and Hume have been at each other's throats from day one. We're just one big happy family up here, and that's not all of it. Tim Loomis is the CIA station chief. He doesn't approve of my posting, and works very hard keeping a wall between us. Cooperation isn't in his vocabulary. He's just going to love you."

"So we'll work around him. Tell me about Jules Carreau."

"He's a brilliant kid," Jean said. "He seems to favor his father's line, but he's going through a radical stage right now. He's eighteen—it's only natural."

Carter grunted agreement. "I remember reading that the prime minister was really left wing in his student days."

Jean nodded. "He'd been to the Soviet Union three times by the age of twenty, and he went into politics before he was thirty."

"Does he still lean to the left?"

"Not so you'd notice. I think it was just a youthful phase."

Carter crushed his cigarette out in the car's ashtray. "What about the local police?"

"Now, that's where you might have a little luck," Jean answered promptly. "Walt Tanks is the chief of police here in Ottawa. Fred Saunders is the chief of the OPP, the Ontario Provincial Police. Tanks has claimed jurisdiction and that's been upheld. Saunders is a friend of Tanks's and has offered his CID people."

"How do they feel about us—about American help in this?"

Jean shrugged. "Indifferent. Unless we get in the way seriously, we can have some latitude. Ambassador Niles knows more about that."

Carter stared out the window for a while, digesting all that he'd just heard. He had a lot of work to do, and only twelve days in which to do it. He couldn't afford to waste a minute.

THREE

The boy stood beside the matron, wanting to hold her hand, her dress, anything to give him courage, but he knew he couldn't. He had to be brave. They had taught him to be brave, but the couple standing in front of him looked so severe. He hugged a stuffed bear to his breast and sought comfort from his small friend.

The woman was stick-slim. She held herself stiffly, her mouth a straight line through compressed lips. Her forehead, under a tightly wound braid of mouse-colored hair, was furrowed. Her eyes, green orbs staring at him through wire-rimmed glasses, seemed cruel.

The man was shorter and rounder. He didn't look fat, just round and hard. He was dressed in dirty overalls still streaked with sheep dung. The boy had heard the man explain that he didn't have time or money for frivolous pursuits. He too looked mean. His bullet head was without a single hair. His ears were close to his head as if afraid to stray. The lines across his forehead and at his mouth were formed from long hours of venting displeasure.

The boy had been told that this second set of parents would teach him discipline and hard work in his new land. It would last a year—more if he needed it. Maybe they would be better than they looked. The last couple had been cruel, the ones who had brought him out during the fighting in someplace called Hungary. They had locked him in a basement closet at night, beating him, overworking him. At the school deep in the Urals where he'd been trained before immigrating to Québec, they'd told him it would be difficult, but it was all for the good of the party.

He couldn't remember when he'd not been at the school. He'd been an orphan. In a wide sweep, looking for talent, Directorate S of the First Chief Directorate, the Illegals Directorate responsible for placing agents under deep cover in strategic positions throughout the world, had tested him. He'd scored so high, they planned for his future as if he were a national treasure. He spent three interminable years at the first school. He could field strip a Kalashnikov with the best of them. They'd taught him about grenades, how to make a crude bomb or a Molotov cocktail, how to infiltrate. But most of all they'd told him of the "Canada plan," although they never gave him all the details. He'd learned English and French until he was accent-free in both languages. He was a jewel in the crown of the Komitet Gosu-darstvennoy Bezopasnosti, the KGB.

From the beginning, he knew that he would live with three couples in Canada at different times. They never told him why. The last would be upper middle class, cultured, politically active. He would be a nephew they adopted when the second couple were killed in an accident. His papers would be in perfect order. He would be schooled by his new parents, constantly supervised, moved carefully through early political affiliations, and finally run for office in a backwater community in Québec.

He would be knowledgeable, cultured, and through the auspices of Directorate S, his parents would have become moderately rich. When the Directorate, or some mysterious control he had not met, thought the time was ripe, his parents would disappear in a boating accident, leaving him a comfortable estate and a perfect background. From the time of their deaths, he would be on a loose rein. His Soviet control would be available but not obtrusive. . . .

As he woke now in the luxurious bedroom, his wife beside him, he smiled, as he did every day upon awakening. He was in a world of his own, a false world, yet in the real world he was a man of power, respected by his community and throughout the country.

He looked ahead to the job at hand. Parisant was dead. His death had been engineered with skill, possibly by Directorate S. He had no way of knowing. His own plans had been advanced by the killing. Parisant had been in the way. The uproar would be loud and long, but Jules would not suffer. They would not be able to pin Parisant's death on Carreau's son and he would be released. He made a mental note to get word out that the boy was to be off limits.

Nick Carter arrived at the embassy in a cab. Thomas Niles had someone with him. His secretary introduced herself.

"I'm Nancy Flanders. I've been with Ambassador Niles on his last three postings," she said, holding out a hand. She was overweight, on the far side of forty-five, and undeniably plain.

But Carter saw beyond the outer woman. The hazel eyes were alert. An intelligent woman lurked behind those eyes, a woman he knew it would be wise to cultivate as a friend. She'd make one hell of an enemy.

"So you're the new military attaché," she said, appraising him. "Welcome to Ottawa, Commander Carlson. I was under the impression you weren't due for a few weeks."

Before Carter could answer, the door opened and Niles was showing a man out. "Commander Carlson?" Niles said, holding out a hand. "Meet Tim Loomis, one of my advisers."

Loomis held out a hand. Carter took it. The two men sized each other up as only two professionals could. Neither had a doubt that the other was some kind of spook. Carter had the advantage of Loomis; Jean had filled him in. Loomis would have to depend on his instincts. Typical of the breed, neither man spoke. They nodded, their handshake lasting only a second or two.

Then Carter was inside and receiving a hearty handshake behind the closed door. "I'm very happy to have you here, whoever you are," Niles said, smiling as he slipped behind his desk.

Carter decided to listen.

"That sounds strange, I know. I asked the president personally for the best man he could send. I didn't want more CIA involvement or help from any other agency controlled by the DCI," he explained quickly.

He was a man who did everything quickly. While he talked at a rapid pace, his hands were busy with papers on his desk, his eyes roamed over Carter missing nothing, and the foot folded over one knee was beating time to a silent rhythm. The ambassador was above average height, handsome in a boyish way, yet gray at the temples. Carter imagined that women found him attractive.

"And here you are, some kind of superspook from an agency that even I haven't heard of," he concluded.

"It has its advantages. What have you told your staff?"

"Nothing. You are what you say you are. Navy records back up your story."

"And Nancy Flanders?"

"She knows no more than anyone else."

"Is this room clean?"

"Loomis has it swept twice a day."

"And you trust Loomis, of course."

Niles took a key from his desk and unlocked a drawer. He took out an electronic sweeper, state of the art, flipped the switch, and moved around the room with professional ease. It was luxurious, as the office of an American ambassador should be. Original oils were hung strategically, subtly lighted. Several groupings of chairs were spotted throughout the huge room. A fireplace, unlit, surrounded by shelves holding hundreds of leather-bound books took up one whole wall.

"That's very good. But anyone can find it in your desk."

"No one has. I've got my own security system," Niles

said with a grin. "I also have a backup and I use it every second day."

"So you don't trust Loomis."

Niles went to a side table and poured two coffees. "How do you take yours?" he asked.

"Black."

"Loomis might be the best they have," Niles answered, returning to his desk with two cups on a laquered tray, "but I don't trust the Company. There have been too damned many foul-ups—too many men playing god."

Carter couldn't agree more. He'd worked with a lot of good CIA types, but he'd met too many who were off center. He agreed with Niles. In something as delicate as this, you didn't want a bull in your china shop. "What about the Canadians?" he asked.

"I assumed you'd been briefed."

"I prefer to hear it from you."

Niles smiled enigmatically. He was a veteran of the diplomatic wars and obviously pleased to deal with a man of Carter's caliber.

"It's not a good situation. It's too bad, really. I think James Turner is a good sort. But he's not Carreau's man and that's two strikes against him before he ever came to bat," Niles said, sipping his coffee. "He'd slipped as an administrator before Carreau came to power. One of his deputies was running his department like the Gestapo. Two cases ended up in the Supreme Court with all the attendant publicity."

"And Turner took the flack."

"The boss man usually does."

"Is he basically a good guy?"

"I think so, but the image is gone, so his teeth are pulled."

"Tell me about Hume."

"Carreau's man. Or he was. The prime minister has a majority so strong it's almost vulgar. He managed to get a bill passed to form a secret service of his own to replace the RCMP CID people. They have almost unlimited power."

"Not very democratic," Carter muttered.

"Hume put himself in trouble almost right away. With the new Bill of Rights here, every lawyer is tying to make a name for himself testing it."

"I don't see how the PM got the bill past the senate."

"There you go. We haven't bothered to understand their politics enough—until now, that is," Niles said, walking to the table and refilling his cup. He moved with the same urgency even when carrying a full cup of coffee. "The senate is a pork-barrel mechanism. The members are appointed by the current prime minister. Only once to my knowledge has the senate opposed a bill."

"Rubber-stamp politics."

"Something like that. It helps explain the possibility of the SSS in a democracy," Niles said, then switched the subject. "The local police are damanding jurisdiction in the Parisant killing. The park where he was found is within their territory. They have Jules Carreau in one of their jails."

"Where? Do you know?"

"Albert Street near Bank. Three blocks from here."

"Do you know the local people?"

"I trust Walter Tanks completely. Walt's a man with unquestioned integrity in my book."

"He's the chief?"

"Right. Fred Saunders is commissioner of the Ontario Provincial Police. That's like our state police."

"How do they get along?"

"The usual departmental jealousies," Niles said, "but I trust Fred Saunders. He's a good cop. Walt trusts him too. Use him if you have to."

"Will you contact them?"

"I will now that I've met you," Niles replied.

Thomas M. T. Niles was a career diplomat, but diplomacy had not always been his strong suit. In the late sixties he'd been a shavetail lieutenant. He'd been assigned to a Captain Charlie Beckwith shortly after Beckwith returned from Bradbury Lines in England after a year with the Special Air Service's 22nd Regiment. At the time, they had been the best antiterrorist fighting force in the world. Beckwith was filled with hope for the immediate formation of an even better American force. It would take more than fifteen years of disappointment, interservice rivalries, and political interference before he'd finally formed Delta Force.

But the first few months with Beckwith had been an eye-opener to Niles. He'd learned more ways to kill in two short months than he'd ever dreamed possible. He was a language specialist. Beckwith had great hopes for him. But a fall on the difficult obstacle course at Beckwith's base had finished a promising career. Niles still walked with a slight limp, one leg shorter than the other.

Now he looked up at the man in front of him as Carter prepared to leave. The brown eyes across the desk met his for a moment and he saw the kind of man he hadn't seen since he left Beckwith. He suppressed a shudder.

Tim Loomis sat in a small office at the rear of the building on the first floor. It was lined with metal mesh, a perfect foil for listening devices. When he or one of his people swept Niles's office twice a day, they then used their detectors on this office, their general office, and their communications room.

Loomis was everyone's image of the perfect CIA man. He was tall and athletic, his dark hair perfectly groomed, his conservative suit immaculate. He had just hung up from talking to Nancy Flanders and he was furious. Niles had informed her that Commander Carlson had permission to carry a gun. The Navy man had no right to carry arms! He was here as an observer! Damn! Something stank here, he thought. For Niles to issue such an order meant that he didn't trust his own chief of station to handle the Carreau situation. It also confirmed his suspicions that Carlson was one hell of a lot more than he was supposed to be.

"Frank!" he shouted. "Get your butt in here!"

Frank Brown was a black man, Loomis's second in command. He was tall and handsome, usually in a good mood, but he wasn't smiling at the curt summons. He stood in front of Loomis's desk without speaking.

"You heard we've got a new naval attaché?"

"In three weeks, yes."

"He's already here. Something about him having two

weeks' leave and deciding to spend it getting to know Ottawa."

"The guy's either too damned eager for his own good, he's nuts, or he's not what he's supposed to be."

Loomis looked up at his colleague. Brown was smart. He'd go a long way in the Company. But right now Brown was second in command. Loomis wasn't the kind to care whether a man might be his boss someday and act accordingly. He dealt with the here and now.

"I want some of our people on this guy. I want to know where he goes and what he does."

"We're spread thin now, Tim. What's so hot about this guy?"

"I've just been told by Mr. High and Mighty that the guy will be armed at all times. How do you like that shit? And he's going to clear it with Tanks and Saunders."

"So I was right. He's not what he's supposed to be."

"I knew that before I called you in here, asshole. Just what the hell do you think he is?"

"He could be G-2. I can check that out. Wouldn't be the first time I've seen a G-2 type working in civilian clothes, carrying a piece," Brown said, his brow furrowed. "He's got to be something special, maybe one of the superspooks we've heard about."

"Well, I want people on him at all times. I want his room at the hotel bugged. I want him assigned a pool car and I want it wired for sound and direction. I want this guy blanketed."

"If he's special, won't he have some heavy clout?" Brown asked, leaning his hands on the desk.

"I don't give a shit. If the flack comes down, it comes

down. In the meantime, I don't want him to fart without my knowing. You get that bastard on tape, you hear?"

Brown left the office and went back to his cubicle with a thoughtful frown on his face. He'd been with the Company for five years, had climbed fast, but had never run into anything like this. He was no fool. He knew that secret agencies existed and he knew why. The Company was too big and unwieldy. It had too many men like Loomis in control. The guy he'd been told to put a blanket over was probably here on direct presidential order. Sure. It made sense. The American president and the Canadian prime minister were good friends. Carreau had probably asked for help. With Turner and Hume to deal with, Brown would have done the same thing.

Carreau hadn't called Niles for Loomis's help. He'd called the Oval Office and this new guy showed up.

So what the hell am I *supposed to do about it?* Brown wondered. If he crossed Loomis, he'd be in the smelly brown stuff up to his knees and he wasn't well enough established to take the flack. Talk to Niles? If that backfired, he'd be in it up to his neck. Talk to the new guy, what was his name? Carlson?

If he was right and the president sent the guy up here, there was no way he was going to mess him up. Shit! Like his daddy used to say: "Nothin's ever easy, son. Not one damned thing's ever easy."

FOUR

Carter left Niles's office, nodded to Nancy Flanders, and was about to leave the embassy, when a tall black man stopped him. He was about Carter's height, outweighed him by twenty pounds, and from the fit of his dark suit, the poundage was all muscle.

"Tim Loomis would like to see you," the man said. "I'm Frank Brown, Mr. Loomis's assistant."

Carter took the hand that was offered. His senses picked up a special message from this man, senses that were an integral part of the Killmaster's bag of tricks, a kind of antennae that never failed him. He picked up two things: one, the assistant station chief didn't like Loomis; and two, he was available as a bypass to CIA help.

He shook the hand warmly, sending out his own message. "Nicholas Carlson. I'll be working here full-time in three weeks."

"They tell me you're on vacation now," Brown said, leading Carter back to the CIA offices. "Seems to me you'd choose a better place."

"You married?" Carter asked.

37

"Yes. Got two kids."

"So we don't think alike. I've got no ties and I've done the Club Med scene and the European fleshpots," Carter lied. "I thought Ottawa would be a welcome change."

"If you need help with your 'welcome change,' let me know," Brown chuckled.

They'd reached Loomis's office. The chief of station didn't get up or offer a hand. He looked busy, which was his specialty whether he was busy or not, and he looked annoyed. Carter couldn't tell if Loomis was perpetually annoyed or whether his standing there was the cause of the man's irritation. He knew he'd find out soon enough.

"We won't need you on this, Frank."

When they were alone, Loomis wasted no time. "What are you doing here?" he demanded.

Carter wasn't impressed by the man or the obvious antisurveillance gadgets surrounding him. He'd met too many good men to be fooled by a phony. The good ones went about their jobs quietly, didn't draw attention to themselves, and kept the tools of their trade out of sight. But he decided to play out his hand and act the innocent.

"Vacation. You've got a problem with that?"

"The problem is, it's all bullshit."

Carter sat back in his chair and put his face in neutral.

"What's this shit about you carrying?" Loomis snapped.

"A habit. How often do you travel light?"

"We're talking about you, not me."

"I don't want trouble, Loomis, but I've got clearance and that's it for me."

"You keep your nose clean, you hear? I don't want to

hear about you coming within a mile of my operation. You got that straight?"

Carter hoisted himself out of his chair. "I can see we're going to work well together," he said. "See you around."

The police building at Albert and Bank streets was a two-story building separated from its closest neighbor by an empty lot. While it was downtown, the streets were almost deserted after dark. The area was quiet until a long line of chanting protesters marched along Albert from the War Memorial where Parisant had been killed. Each man and woman carried a torch overhead. The shadows cast by the flames painted weird shadows on the empty buildings as they passed.

Police on duty came out to see what was going on. The marchers came on, slowly, until they had surrounded the building.

"Send him out!" one of the men shouted in French. "We want the killer of Gilles Parisant! Do it now!"

They all began to chant at once: "We want Carreau! We want Carreau! We want Carreau!"

The chant continued until a sergeant came out of the front door with a shotgun. He fired both barrels into the night sky and shouted at the marchers in both English and French. "You will all be arrested for disturbing the peace if you don't disburse."

They didn't hear him over the noise they were making. But the shotgun had its effect. Some of the men reached inside their shirts and two of the women slipped their hands under their skirts. They came out with wine bottles filled with gasoline. Each bottle had a rag stuffed down the neck.

The action was uncoordinated but effective. Torches were dipped to the wicks of the Molotov cocktails and the bottles were thrown at the building. Some broke against the brick walls and spread flame in all directions. Others hit the bars of the windows and spread flame across the glass to drip off the sills to the street. Two or three missed the bars and crashed through the glass. The police outside had to duck inside for cover as flames roared about them.

As if on signal, the crowd took off running. They were in groups of eight or ten. Far enough down the streets to avoid detection, pickup trucks pulled into view and raced away with the demonstrators.

The police building, a downtown precinct with its own jail, was an inferno within seconds.

Carter passed Brown's office on the way out. The big man waved him in. "You get the standard lecture?" he asked, his handsome face split by a grin.

"I think he embellished it some," Carter said, preparing to sit.

The phone rang and Brown answered it. His forehead furrowed and his expression changed. "Shit! Where they got him?"

He waited for an answer and slammed the phone down.

"What is it?" Carter asked as Brown headed for the door.

"Separatists set fire to the jail where they've got Carreau."

Carter took off after Brown. They hopped into an agency car that was in a diplomatic parking spot and were moving within ten seconds of the call. The ride took all of one minute before they pulled up on the other side of the street from the flaming building.

It was too soon for a crowd to have formed. The fire department sirens could be heard in the distance. Brown and Carter raced into the front door. The heat was almost unbearable.

"Where's Carreau?" Brown asked a sergeant who was held back by the flames.

"In back. Second floor. We need masks and tanks to get through the smoke. The fire department—"

Carter took off running to the back of the building. He opened a door momentarily and took in deep lungsful of air. Through long years of yoga practice, he had trained himself to hold his breath for four minutes or more.

The back stairwell was almost free of smoke but was filling fast. The smoke worked on his eyes until they were watering so much he could barely see. Carter took the stairs two at a time and ran into an officer who was walking in circles, holding a handkerchief to his eyes.

"Where's Carreau?" he shouted, losing the precious breath he'd been holding.

"Who the hell are you?" the man rasped.

"I've got to save Carreau. Where is he?"

"He's down at the end of the corridor. I couldn't get to him. I'm not giving him up—" The man coughed deep from his gut. "You could be the one who started—" He couldn't finish as the smoke filled his lungs.

Carter grabbed the keys from the man's belt and raced down the corridor as the officer toppled over.

His lungs burned but he couldn't get any air until this was over. A wall of fire spread across the corridor in front of him where a guard's desk and chair burned furiously. All of the cells were empty. He reasoned that nothing could be feeding the fire on the other side if only cells occupied the rest of the floor.

Carter ran through the flames suffering nothing more than singed hair and eyebrows. Within seconds he was through and in another area of cells, but he saw no one.

At the far end, a figure was sprawled on the floor of a cell. Carter tried three keys before he found the right one. He didn't waste a second. His lungs were burning fiercely and his head throbbed as the lack of oxygen starved his brain.

He hoisted the young man in a fireman's carry and ran back the way he had come. The wall of fire was worse than before. The desk was one mass of flame, the wood crackling as it expanded and split.

Carter didn't hesitate. The added weight was taxing his strength. He rushed through, tripping over the chair he couldn't see in the flames. He and his burden hit the terrazzo floor and skidded ten feet before they were stopped by a body.

The air was better near the floor. The Killmaster knew this, but he had to carry Jules Carreau out and crawling wasn't going to do it. He felt for a pulse, first Carreau, then the officer. They were both alive. He hoisted Carreau on his shoulder and dragged the officer to the stairs.

His head was spinning. He had lost all sense of direction. Even with his stamina, the task was too much.

As he took the first step down, he lost his balance. The three bodies tumbled to the bottom and lay still.

He couldn't remember when he'd been so mad. In all the years he'd worked carefully to improve his position and preserve his identity, he'd never seen anything handled as badly as this. For the Carreau boy to have been killed would have damaged their cause. The undecided votes in Québec, the Anglos who were too lazy to fight the referendum, the new immigrants who didn't want to take sides, they would all have been swayed by such foolishness.

He went to his bedroom to make the call. As he keyed in the number, he idly fondled a small stuffed animal on the bed.

"Oui?" a voice answered.

"You fool! Trying to kill the Carreau boy could have ruined us!"

"Try? Isn't he dead?"

"No. He's in hospital. Didn't you get my message?"

"Yes, but I thought . . . you know . . . I thought with him out of the way . . . so dramatic a death . . . the party would rally around us."

"We have the party, you fool! If he'd been killed, too many undecided votes could have swung the wrong way. Don't you ever use your head?"

"I just thought—"

"I'll tell you what to think about. If you ever pull anything against my orders again . . . if you ever pull anything like that again without checking with me first, you are a dead man. You got that? A dead man!"

He slammed down the phone and sat for a moment

breathing hard. It would all be over for him soon. One man could accomplish just so much. He'd undermined the RCMP and the SSS. He'd brought the referendum to a head. When they won, he would have been at the game long enough. It would be time for him to disappear, time for the KGB to stage a fake accident for him.

Before he went back downstairs to his family, he wondered how he would be mourned in Canada after his death. It would be great sport to see the funeral, hear the eulogies, and know the irony.

The first thing Carter felt when he opened his eyes was a burning in his throat. He tried to put his hand to it, but the hand was bandaged.

"You're awake," a sweet voice sounded near his ear. "How do you feel?"

"Water," he croaked.

"I've got a mixture you should swallow slowly. It will soothe your throat."

"Where am I?"

"St. Vincent's Hospital. We were the closest," the nurse said.

Another body in white loomed over him. A flashlight was shone in one eye than the other. "How do you feel?" the doctor asked.

"All right. My throat is pretty raw."

"It's a damned miracle you're alive at all."

He was interrupted by Thomas Niles who'd come rushing in as soon as he heard voices. "How is he, Doctor?" he asked, almost out of breath.

"Fine. He's going to be all right, Mr. Ambassador," the doctor said. "It's a miracle if you ask me. Sore

throat, but no damage to the lungs. Singed hair, super-
ficial burns to the backs of his hands. That's it."

Niles came to stand beside Carter and smiled. "You
did a fine job, Commander. One hell of a fine job."

"How's Carreau?" Carter whispered. He knew his
voice would not be the same for a few days.

"Remarkably well. He's not as well as you, but he'll
recover fully with a few days in here."

"What about the other one?" Carter asked. His brain
was fuzzy on details. "I seem to remember another one."

"He's better than both of you. Sitting on the edge of
his bed telling his chief that you saved his life."

Carter waved off the comment with a bandaged hand.
"Keep the photographers away from me. I can't . . ."

"I understand. No pictures," Niles said. "The only
bad part of this is the spotlight on the hero. Hard to
avoid, I'm afraid."

"The only way is for you to get me out of here
secretly." Carter pulled off the bandages and examined
his hands. They were blistered but not badly burned. He
walked to the small washroom and looked at his face,
holding the open back of the hospital gown with one
hand.

The singed eyebrows weren't bad and the singed hair
would be easy to correct with a razor blade. "I'm getting
dressed," he announced. "Will you arrange a car, sir?"

"Not so fast. The prime minister is down the hall
visiting his boy. He wants to see you."

"Won't the press trail after him?"

"I suppose you're right."

"He's the one who called the president in the first

place. Carreau's got to know how important it is for me to keep in the background."

"There's a reception at his home tomorrow night. I'll introduce you there," Niles said. "Wear your dress whites. And, Carlson, you did one hell of a job tonight."

Carter slipped into the nondescript car that was parked out back. Brown was driving. "How's the hero?"

"Stuff it, Frank. Let's get out of here, okay? I've got one hell of a headache and a throat that feels like it's been barbecued."

"How about some twenty-year-old scotch?"

"Sounds like it might be a solution."

"I know the bell captain at your hotel. No sweat," Brown said. He concentrated on his driving as he turned off Bronson Avenue, past the spires of Christ Church Cathedral, on to Spark Street and finally Wellington. The morning traffic rush was over. They circled the War Memorial and slipped into the hotel driveway in minutes.

"You're in Walt Tanks's good books, Carlson. Man, I've never seen a man so happy with anyone."

"The guy just lost a precinct house," Carter said as they climbed the six steps to the door held by a uniformed doorman.

"An old relic of a building. The point is, he didn't lose a man, thanks to you. And he'd have been in it up to his hips if the kid had been fried."

"You've got a way with words, you know that?" Carter said, grinning.

Brown chuckled. "Just trying to make you feel better. Anyway, one drink and I've got to get back. Our friend

Loomis is a class-A bastard. He's pissed off that I took you with me last night. Now you're the fair-haired boy and he can't ride herd on you."

"He tell you to call off my surveillance?"

"How did you . . . ?"

"It figures. I can't work with a tap on my phone and the room bugged, Frank," Carter said, his voice sounding more normal with use. "Can you arrange that?" He had no intention of worrying about listening devices. He'd use Jean Sprague's setup at the embassy to call Hawk, and her apartment for most other calls. If they tried to follow him to her place, they'd get one rude awakening.

"Can do. You see the PM yet?"

"I'm supposed to see him at a reception tomorrow night, or is it tonight? I'm still a little confused. Have to check with Niles."

Brown stayed for a drink, tried to pry information out of Carter about his past, and finally took off.

Carter took off his shoes and lay back on the bed, setting his mental alarm for one hour. He closed his eyes and was asleep in seconds.

FIVE

The scene at 24 Sussex Drive was in sharp contrast to the morning Gilles Parisant was driven to his death. Cars lined the long circular drive. Car jockeys worked furiously to relieve owners of their vehicles or direct chauffeurs to parking in the rear. Scores of men in business suits helped with the traffic or stood at strategic locations, their eyes scanning the arrivals.

The house was ablaze with lights. Carter realized it wasn't intended to fulfill the functions of the White House. Many official functions, the biggest, most impressive ones, were held at the home of the Governor General, the Queen's official representative. The official functions at Sussex Drive were more intimate, less formal, with lower-echelon embassy people.

Jacques and Marie Carreau were near the front door, not obviously greeting guests, but close by to catch the eye of the ones they especially wanted to talk with. The game of politics was never-ending.

Carter entered with Jean Sprague on his arm. He was in dress whites with a chest full of ribbons. Jean had

49

decided to wear a formal gown, her reasoning being that a couple in uniform would look too stiff. He decided she had done it out of vanity and he was glad. She was an asset to any man, a beauty, and particularly attractive in the long black sheath that was cut low in the back *and* in the front.

Jean pointed out the prime minister and his wife. Marie Carreau was wearing a marigold-yellow gown that contrasted beautifully with her dark hair. Carter remembered what Jean had told him in the car, about Marie and the deputy prime minister. She was definitely an attractive woman.

Ambassador Niles was at Carter's elbow as they moved ahead with the crowd. He guided them to the Carreaus after only a brief welcome and a compliment to Jean.

The prime minister of Canada looked directly into the eyes of the man from AXE as they were introduced. He seemed to have the ability to shut out the world when he wanted to concentrate on one person. Carter had noted the same ability in the president. Up close, he could see the fatigue lines around the man's eyes and mouth, a trait shared by men with too much responsibility.

"You are the man who saved our boy," he said, his voice showing emotion.

Marie Carreau's eyes widened at the statement. Her face blanched as her gloved hand went to her mouth. Then she cupped Carter's face gently in her hands and kissed him on one cheek, then the other. Her eyes were moist. It was an emotional moment for her. "Thank you. Thank you," she said, her voice cracking. "I don't even know who you are."

"Commander Nicholas Carlson of the United States Navy, my dear," Carreau recited. "And if I'm not mistaken, this is Commander Sprague."

"I'm so grateful," Marie went on, taking his hand. She turned it over and saw the ugly red blisters Carter had been trying to hide. "I'm sorry, Jacques," she said, her voice breaking. "I have to go to my room for a moment. "If anything had happened . . ."

"I understand," the prime minister said as she turned to leave. "Come with me, Commander Carlson," Carreau said quietly. "I'd like to see you alone."

Carter followed the leader of the Canadian people to a small den not far from the main reception hall.

"I think it best if we speak alone," Carreau said. "I'm sorry, my dear."

"Jean is my colleague, sir. I don't believe anything we will talk about is out of her field."

"As you wish," he said, leading them into a cozy, book-lined den. "A drink?" he asked.

"Scotch," Carter said. "Two cubes."

"And you, Commander?"

"That will be fine."

The prime minister poured for them and sat in a large winged chair. "My call to your president has paid off already. Even if you can't help with the murder of my friend, you have done more than I can ever repay."

"Forget it, sir. What can you tell me about the man who will succeed Parisant?"

"Guy Lafontaine? He'll be more difficult to deal with, more militant."

"Do you think he might have been behind the attempt on your son?"

Carreau thought about the question as he sipped his drink. "He's never been convicted of a crime, but . . ."

"But what?" Carter prodded.

"I've always thought he was behind some of the early separatist activity . . . the bombings in the sixties."

"It seems to me he's got the most to gain by Parisant's death. Is his position secure?" Carter said. He glanced at Jean. She seemed content to listen for the moment.

"He has opposition, but I believe he can ride it out," Carreau said. "He's already been confirmed as the interim leader."

"What about your second in command?"

"Robert? What about him?" Carreau asked, his brow furrowing for the first time.

"Robert Boisvert. I've studied our files on him. He seems too good to be true," Carter said. "Sometimes the pillars, the lily-white ones, they're the ones with most to hide."

"Does your file show any flaws?" Carreau asked, his voice rising slightly.

"No," Carter admitted. He knew he was on thin ice here and he veered off. "I can see that both Turner and Hume would have scores to settle with you, but I don't see what killing Parisant would do to help them."

"They're both good men, Commander Carlson. Misguided perhaps, infatuated with power, but both good men."

"But either man could do you irreparable harm by killing Parisant," Carter countered.

"Perhaps. But is revenge enough? It seems to me that power, an increase in stature, would be more of a motive," Carreau said, putting down his glass and pulling at his beard thoughtfully. "Attempting to kill my son was the act of a stupid man," he said after a long delay.

"I've got my own theories on that," Carter said. "Care to explain?"

"I think I can explain it," Jean broke in for the first time. "Killing Mr. Parisant might rally the hard-core separatists around the party, but they would have gone to the polls anyway. Something with far more effect on the referendum would have been the death of Jules Carreau."

"How do you figure that?" Carter asked.

Carreau just sat back, his eyes on Jean admiringly.

"I've followed the polls carefully. The Liberal party in Québec is Mr. Carreau's best tool. They have thirty percent of the vote while the separatists have forty. That leaves thirty percent undecided with eight days to go."

"Nine," Carreau corrected. "But you are on track. Go ahead."

"The callous murder of Jules by separatists might jog the undecided voters, the Anglos who are holding back, the ethnic populations who have kept out of it."

"While the death of Parisant would not?" Carter asked.

"No one would believe that the prime minister would be stupid enough to kill Parisant, an old friend, to swing the vote," she said.

"So who's our best bet?" Carter asked.

"I think Mr. Carreau has an enemy he doesn't recognize—a brilliant enemy. But that doesn't explain the blunder at the jail," she went on. "Maybe the mastermind has stupid lieutenants. It's happened before."

"Too far-fetched. Who would the mastermind be?" Carreau asked, drinking the last of his scotch.

"I don't know," Jean admitted. "It's all theory. But I don't think the man—or woman—who arranged for the killing of Gilles Parisant is someone obvious."

"I'd like to meet Lafontaine and Boisvert," Carter said. "Are they here?"

"They are," Carreau said, getting to his feet.

"I know them. Perhaps it would be less obvious if I introduced you," Jean said, also rising, following Carreau's lead.

"What about Turner and Hume?"

"They are here. Do you know them, Commander Sprague?" the prime minister asked. She nodded. "I agree it would be better, less obvious, if you introduced the commander."

They entered the main hall without Carreau. He left from a different door to make their meeting less obvious.

"That's Robert Boisvert with Marie Carreau," Jean said, steering them toward the couple.

Marie Carreau had completely recovered her composure. Her eyes were shining as she talked animatedly to Boisvert. The man was younger than Carter expected, somewhere in his early forties, with dark brown hair and a wide face.

As they approached, Boisvert's dark blue eyes focused on them. Here was another man of authority, Carter thought. He had the same look of extreme confidence a president or a prime minister would have. One other thing was obvious. He did not have their look of fatigue, the look that spoke of overwhelming concerns. On the contrary, his face was unlined as if he hadn't a care in the world.

"Oh, Robert!" Marie exclaimed as they approached. She pronounced the name in the French way, Ro-*bare*. "This is Commander Carlson, the man who saved my Jules. A real hero."

Boisvert turned his intense gaze on Carter, sizing him up. No sign of either gratitude or recognition was present. The look was entirely neutral, which seemed strange to Carter at this stage. Boisvert held out a hand. "Well done, Commander." He had uttered the words for Carter, but his eyes were on Jean.

"And this is another commander," Marie said, her introductions uncertain for a woman in her position. "May I introduce Commander Jean Sprague. She is with the American embassy."

"Such responsibility for one so beautiful," Boisvert said, taking her hand and bringing his lips close to it.

"Are you against women in the service, Mr. Boisvert?" Jean asked.

"I'm not a chauvinist, if that's what you mean." Boisvert countered. "It just seems such a waste."

"That, Mr. Boisvert, qualifies you eminently," she said, laughing. "I'm surprised at you, a politician."

With the last word on the subject she led Carter away to an uncrowded part of the room. They picked up cups of punch on the way.

"She's in love with him," she announced in a whisper.

"What?" he exclaimed. It was the last thing he expected to hear. "How could you know?"

"Female telegraph. I don't need another woman to tell me. Marie managed that by herself."

Carter was not immune to any emotion. He'd seen it all. But he was surprised. What Marie Carreau was doing was dynamite. He had to sort out the motivations of such a liaison. Who started it? Who had most to gain? It put Boisvert in the running for a full investigation.

"Carlson!" a voice boomed from behind them. At the same time, a huge hand slapped Carter on the back, spilling half his cup of punch on the light gray carpet.

Carter turned to see a bear of a man standing over him. He was well past fifty, his hair in a crew cut, his shoulders massive, but in proportion his belly won hands down. The craggy face was smiling, showing even yellow teeth. "Chief Tanks. You saved my ass."

A second man was with the chief of police. He hung back until Tanks had his say. He looked more like an intellectual, his narrow face partly concealed behind old-fashioned black-rimmed glasses. His penetrating eyes were an eerie light green.

"This here's Fred Saunders," the loud voice of the chief went on, brooking no interruption. "Good friend. He heads up the Ontario Provincial Police.

Carter couldn't take the hand offered by Saunders. His own was captured in the huge paw that had clapped him on the back. Tanks held on to it while he went on about what the rescue had meant to him, how grateful he was, and if there was anything he could do . . . They said all the trite things and the big man finally let go of Carter's hand.

Saunders took it and shook it with care. Carter noted that the man had seen the damage from the fire and was not about to cause him pain. He suspected that not much was missed by those green eyes.

"I echo Walt's feelings. We'd have had one mess on our hands without your intervention."

"I was in the right spot at the right time. Anyone could have done it."

"Bullshit!" Saunders said, sounding completely out of character for the moment. "If I can ever do anything for you, you damn well let me know."

"I will."

"I'm available to you, Commander. I don't imagine how I could ever help you, but if I can . . ."

Jean steered him away. "I think we'll take Chief Tanks in small doses," she whispered into his ear as she clung to his arm. "Oh. There's Lafontaine. I don't know the crowd he's with. You want to barge in?"

While she asked the question, the crowd around Guy Lafontaine left him. Carter wheeled Jean over to the older man before he was surrounded by well-wishers again. It wasn't every week that a man was elevated to a seat of power that controlled a population the size of New York City.

"Mr. Lafontaine," Carter said. "May I present Commander Jean Sprague of the American embassy?"

"Enchanté, mademoiselle," the acting premier of Québec replied. *"Et vous, monsieur?"*

"I am Commander Carlson, also of the embassy," Carter answered in French, since the leader of the separatists seemed so inclined. "We've both been anxious to meet you."

"Ah. And why is that?" the tall man asked. He was very slim. His clothes seemed to hang as if still on hangers, the points jutting out at his shoulders. He vaguely reminded Carter of a stooped scarecrow. Or a large-beaked crane wearing a suit.

"Your climb to power in Québec has not escaped the attention of our people south of the border," Carter went on. "If you do separate, we are concerned about our relationship."

"And what is your field, Commander?" Lafontaine asked with an edge of sarcasm to his voice.

"Military, sir. But that doesn't stop a man from thinking. What do you think of the Jules Carreau affair?" he suddenly asked, changing the subject.

Carter watched for a reaction and got one. It was almost imperceptible, but it was there. Above the man's large nose, his eyes narrowed slightly with displeasure. The question was whether he just didn't like to talk about the subject, or whether he had anything to do with the act itself.

"He is a lucky young man, which is more than can be said for Parisant. I find the entire matter most distressing."

"Of course," Carter said, letting it drop. Lafontaine fascinated him, as did Boisvert. He had small dossiers on them both but had to learn more. He decided to make a call on both of them at their homes, preferably when they were both away.

He squeezed Jean's arm slightly and started to lead her away. *"Bonne chance,"* he said in parting. "Good luck."

"Pas de chance, Commander," Lafontaine retorted. "Luck has nothing to do with it."

"What was that all about?" Jean asked when they were far enough away.

"Just feeling each other out. He's our main suspect in

the Parisant assassination. He suspects I'm a predator on his trail."

"A perceptive man. He's also a very furtive man. My French is lousy, so I just watched him."

"That one is more than just furtive. I think he's capable of anything. I'll have to find out what makes him tick."

"I see Turner and Hume standing together," Jean said. "Want to corner them now while you have a chance?"

"Let's call it a night. What do you say?" he asked. He wanted some time alone to think about what he'd learned. The idea of unraveling two more complicated characters didn't appeal to him. He'd do some checking on them and meet them at some other time.

If there was time. Time was his enemy now. He had to get to Parisant's killer and do it before the polls opened for the referendum, preferably in time for the evening news the night before.

"Would you like to come over for a nightcap?" Jean said as they waited for their car.

"Can I have a rain check?" he asked. "There's something I've got to do."

"Okay, how about a steak at my place tomorrow night?" she said.

"You're on."

SIX

The car rental desk was still open at Carter's hotel. He obtained the most common model available, got a map of the city, and drove south on Bank Street to Highway 31. It was one of the busiest routes to the airport. Boisvert's estate was south of the airport on the road to Morrisburg. Frank Brown had given him directions.

Carter stopped at a farm lane well out of town and changed into black fatigues. His weapons were strapped in place outside, easy to reach. A powerful flashlight hung from his belt. A small leather case, one of AXE wizard Howard Schmidt's specialties, was in a hip pocket. It contained three vials of drugs: lethal, debilitating, and Pentothol. He also had a pair of Schmidt's laser detectors. They fitted over his eyes like a piece of space traveler's equipment, secured around his head by a strong rubber strap. The most unusual item for him was commonplace, a pair of leather linesman's gloves.

The night sky had been clear when Carter left the center of the city, but it had clouded over in the past half hour. Every few hundred yards he had to use the flashlight at the entrance to one of the estate properties to identify it. They were beginning to line the highway on both sides.

Boisvert's property was closed off to visitors by a pair of steel gates. A gateman's hut stood to one side inside the gates. Its windows were dark. A closed-circuit camera was mounted on a post to the left.

Carter parked in the shadows well away from the gates. Brown had provided no information on Boisvert's security. Since no one was on the gates, Carter assumed the grounds were patrolled by dogs or crisscrossed by lasers.

The fence posed no problem. Inside the grounds he scanned for lasers and found none. He waited for a few minutes, listening. He was not worried about time. He had left the party early. Boisvert would probably stay to the end, but he had no guarantees.

While he was listening, a drumming sound reached him faintly. As the sound increased, it was accompanied by labored breathing. Carter turned to face the sound. He assumed a fighting pose, his legs spread slightly, his knees flexed, his arms held out in front, the fingers spread.

When the attack came, it was lightning fast. With no more than a grunt of effort, the pit bull left the ground and dived for his throat. Carter saw the open mouth, the teeth like a row of spearheads shining in the night.

He reacted instantly. Moving slightly to his left, he caught a paw in his right hand and fell backward as fast as he could. His arm whipped the dog forward, using the canine's weight to propel him against the wall.

The animal was just stunned. Carter was on him

before he could move, pressing the nerves at the side of the powerful neck until the eighty pounds of fury subsided.

The drumming of paws came at him again. This time he wasn't able to maneuver. He grasped both sides of the dog's mouth in his leather gloves and pressed the writhing body against the wall until he could get a hand free to render the dog unconscious.

He fell to his knees breathing heavily. The dogs were stretched out in front of him. He gave himself a few seconds to recover, then carefully injected each animal with enough of the debilitating drug to keep it out of action for an hour. If he couldn't do the job in an hour, he figured, he should switch professions.

Carter pulled himself to his feet and moved out of the shrubbery near the wall. The house was dark except for one light in a second-floor window. The building was a gray stone Tudor, two stories. It looked spacious and the four-car garage to one side added to the appearance of size.

Moving quickly from the wall to the house, Carter examined every room on the ground floor. He saw no one. Completing the circle, looking in the last window, he heard the unmistakable sound of a lighter. A brief flash of light cast a glow on the stone wall near him.

A guard. The man was having a smoke. Carter stepped carefully to the edge of the wall and looked around. A husky man stood in the shadows, his back to the house.

One of Carter's objectives was to leave no clues that the house had been visited. The dogs would recover and show no sign of his presence. The guard was another matter.

The smoker stood next to an arbor. Annuals had been potted in the last few days and hung from the arbor lattice near the man's head. Slowly, Carter crept along the wall. At the last second, he left his feet, catching the man with a karate chop on the way down. He gave the inert form a short dose of the drug, then pulled the largest pot from its hanger, wrapped it with a doormat, and smashed it next to where the man lay.

Again he waited for a few minutes, listening carefully. He heard nothing. The door behind the guard was unlocked. He crept in and made a quick circuit of the lower floor to be sure the guard had no company. Again he detected no lasers, so he folded the uncomfortable goggles and put them away.

Carter stole up the long stairway at the front of the house feeling vulnerable so out in the open. Only one door had a light under it. He grasped the handle and turned slowly, easing the door inward until he could get his head in a position to see. The housekeeper was sitting in a reclining chair, a book loose in her hand, her head against her chest.

He eased the door closed.

Only one other room was occupied. Two children slept in twin beds in one huge room. The clouds had cleared. Moonlight was streaming through flower-patterned curtains. The children slept under the watchful eye of an assortment of stuffed animals, bears and giraffes, camels and pandas, slim and fat animals, old and new animals, in all the colors of the rainbow.

Carter slipped into the master bedroom and went

through a desk and two end tables, careful to leave them as he'd found them. Nothing was obviously out of the ordinary. Nothing except a tattered old stuffed animal that rested against a pillow on the bed.

He slipped downstairs and searched the desk in a room that had to be Boisvert's den. Again he found nothing. He wasn't surprised. Boisvert would be stupid to leave anything incriminating at home. If he was involved in the Parisant affair, he'd have to be very careful.

On the way out, Carter took a minute to go through the guard's pockets. Apart from the usual money and credit cards, all in the name of Karl Jones, he found nothing. The man had a weapon, a police special, again nothing out of the ordinary. One thing was unusual, but it didn't hit Carter right away. The suit, the cloth it was made from, it wasn't exactly North American.

So what was it? While he pondered the mystery, he heard one of the dogs approaching. It was shaking its head from side to side, almost recovered. It seemed to be oblivious of Carter. Instead, it went to the guard and whined, trying to push the man's head so he could lick the face.

The guard groaned. The second dog appeared and growled low in his throat. Headlights appeared at the gate and soon were starting up the drive.

It was time to get out.

On the way to Jean Sprague's apartment the following evening, he picked up a tail and let them follow him until he felt sure they were Loomis's people. Once he was sure the men in the car following him weren't on the other side, he lost them in the market area, knifing through protesting pedestrians and whipping into the Holiday Inn parking lot at George and Dalhousie streets. When the frustrated CIA men passed the lot, trying to pick up his trail, he headed to Jean's using a roundabout route through Rockliffe Park and Manor Park.

He was just turning on to St. Laurent Boulevard a few blocks from the apartment when he noticed a car he'd seen downtown and again in Rockliffe Park. Now it was turning on to St. Laurent with him. Loomis's boys were better than he thought. They must have had at least one parallel car on him, he figured. Carter didn't think Loomis had that kind of manpower.

Carter cut into the Rideau High School parking lot and circled to make sure the lot was empty. With his headlights turned off, he drove back toward the entrance just as the other car turned in.

It was always the same. Two agencies of the same government spending good money fighting each other. Usually he let it go, kept out of their way, but this time he was going to flush them out.

The other car drove alongside. As it passed, an ugly face peered out at him. The face was grinning as a massive hand holding an oversize gun appeared. Two flashes erupted from the gun, but Carter didn't see them. He had rolled to one side and out the other door. As the other car started to turn, he got off three quick shots. One 9mm slug from Carter's Luger ripped through a sleeve and the shooter's gun clattered from a shattered hand. The other two shots sheared through metal at the rear of the car.

The tank blew. The spread of burning fuel was so quick, the two men were engulfed. The doors opened but they didn't appear. Instead, the flaming car careened toward a chain link fence, coming to rest against it, the flames climbing to the night sky.

Carter ran to the gun, picked it up, and headed back to his car. He took off without lights and didn't stop until he was six blocks away in the Belgate Shopping Center parking lot.

He examined the car. Both side windows had been open. The shots must have passed straight through. He examined the gun. He hadn't seen one like it for a long time—a Graz Buyra. They had been popular with the KGB years ago. This one had seen years of hard use. The man who had used it had been an old hand at the game.

Carter wondered if perhaps he'd been too quick to send them to a fiery grave. He could have learned something from them. The encounter brought up a lot of questions. Why was the KGB on to him? Was the tail the result of his visit to Boisvert's house? He remembered Karl Jones's suit. A KGB guard at Boisvert's estate . . . ? Things just didn't make sense.

One bothersome question was Jean's safety. The incident had happened a few blocks from her place. He drove for a half hour, making sure he wasn't followed. Finally, when he felt safe, he spotted a phone booth and pulled over. He dialed Jean's number and she answered on the second ring.

"Something's happened," Carter said as soon as he had her on the line. He told her about the attempt on his life and the KGB gun. He warned her to keep her eyes open and promised to call her the following day.

• • •

"Let me talk to Guy."

"Who shall I say is calling?"

"Just tell him to get his ass to the phone. He'll know who it is."

The caller waited for a few seconds. He was impatient and held his temper in check as well as he could.

"I told you never to call me here," Lafontaine said. He sounded out of breath.

"I'll call you where and when I want," the caller said in Russian. *"Now listen and listen well. Some of your people blew it tonight and they're dead."*

"Dead?" Lafontaine said, still sounding out of breath. It wasn't unusual. He had a tendency to hyperventilate when talking to his control. *"What happened?"*

"They were following the American Navy commander."

"And he killed them?"

"That's how it looks," the caller said at the other end. *"What does that tell you?"*

"That the commander isn't what he's supposed to be. A naval attaché wouldn't get to our people. Not unless he's had special training."

"More than that. He'd think twice about shooting and being killed in the process. This one is good. He's very good."

"What do you want me to do?"

"The glorious new leader of the separatist government of Québec doesn't know what to do," the caller said, his voice dripping with sarcasm. *"You find out who this American is and what he knows. You exploit his weak spots. You do exactly what we trained you to do."*

"What if I'm exposed? I can't take chances now. We're too close."

"Listen well, Guy Lafontaine. If you can't figure out how to neutralize this one man, you are no use to us—none. Now get the hell on with the job, comrade."

The line went dead, leaving one man at the other end, in Québec City, breathing hard and starting to sweat.

"I love you," the woman moaned into his ear as she lay beneath the body of a man in the canopied bed. The bodies were stark white. Neither had seen the sun for months.

"We said we wouldn't talk about love," he growled. It was difficult for him to talk as the sensation filled his loins and threatened to send him over the top too soon.

"Oh, Bobby, I've got to leave him soon," she said, her breath coming in short bursts. "I can't stand not being with you every night."

"Can't . . . Marie . . . not yet," he said, unable to wait any longer. He moved over her, fulfilling the act, sending her to a new height of pleasure while satisfying himself.

They lay together, not speaking, until their breathing returned to normal. It pleased Boisvert that this was the prime minister's bed. It pleased him that Carreau was a fool and still confided in his wife most of his inner thoughts. The man he would replace one day was an unsuspecting ass.

It would be over soon, he told himself. When the separatists made all Carreau's efforts look like the ineffectual attempts of a fool, it would be the beginning of the end for the man who had stood in his way for so long. And it would be the beginning of real power for him, for Robert Boisvert.

He rolled off her, their skin parting reluctantly. She clung to him, pressing the length of her against him.

"What does Jacques plan to do about Lafontaine? Will he try to undermine him in the next few days?" he whispered into her ear.

"I don't want to talk about him now."

"I know. But I have to help him all I can. What has he planned?"

"But I want to talk about us. Will we be together when this is over?"

"Soon after. I promise. I don't want to be apart any more than you."

"Have you talked to your wife?"

"No reason to until Jacques knows."

"I'll tell him when he gets back," she said, her excitement mounting.

"Not yet. Let's get the referendum over with. Just another week."

"Promise?"

"Promise. Now, what about Lafontaine?"

"Jacques isn't worried about Lafontaine. He has another plan. Bernard Fornier has something on Lafontaine. He's going to spring it at the last minute."

"Why didn't you tell me this before?" he said, pulling away from her.

She clung to him. "I just learned last night. Jacques was overwrought . . . you know . . . the horrible thing that happened to Jules. He just blurted it out last night, the business about Fornier."

"Does anyone else know?"

"No. Apparently Fornier has the material in his safe at home. He's saving it for the last minute."

Boisvert let her move her hands over his body while he thought of his next moves. Fornier was the Liberal party leader, the opposition party in Québec. He had a strong following who would vote against the referendum. "What is it they have? Do you know?" he asked.

"He didn't tell me. Really, Bobby, he didn't tell me."

"You must know something . . . some hint."

"Just that it's very bad. Lafontaine's connected to a foreign government in some way. I don't know how."

"How did Fornier come across it?"

"The QPP commissioner. He's a Liberal sympathizer."

"The new one, Georges Plante?"

"No. The one who died last month, the one Plante replaced. Jacques said something about him being the end of the line, whatever that means."

He rolled back over her again and brought his lips to hers. "I don't think I could have been able to stand the pressure here without you, dear Marie," he said, caressing her breasts.

"Oh, Bobby. I can't wait for this whole mess to be over. Promise me I won't have to wait much longer."

"I've never lied to you, my love. It will all be over soon."

SEVEN

With six days to the referendum, Carter was no closer to the solution than he had been the day before. All he knew was that the KGB was involved. And all that told him was that one of the principals was working for them. They'd either turned him, or he'd been in place for a long time.

On his way to talk over their day with Brown at his rural home in a district called Nepean, Carter spotted a car following him along Merivale Road. He took no evasive action, but looked for a place to make a quick move and turn the tables on his pursuers.

The car was a Lincoln Town Car, not uncommon in the capital. Suddenly, the Lincoln veered to the left, pulled alongside Carter's smaller car, and tried to force it off the road.

Carter slipped his Luger into his right hand, but before he was able to open a window, the big car turned sharply to the right. The smaller car's right front wheel caught in a soft shoulder. Despite the Killmaster's effort to stay on the road, the car careened to the right and into a steep ditch.

Dazed from a gut-wrenching blow from the steering wheel, Carter felt strong hands pulling him from the car. He shook his head, mustered all the strength he had, and put everything into a hard right. It met the soft belly of one of his pursuers. As he turned to grapple with the second man, he had only a brief look at the cruel face before something crashed against his skull. His face hit the mud of the ditch and the distant streetlights faded to black.

Consciousness returned slowly, accompanied by one massive headache. He was in the back of a car, face-down, the feet of the two men resting on him. He wasn't sure how far they traveled. In about ten minutes he felt a needle in his left arm just before the car stopped. In a daze, he remembered being pulled from the car and dragged to a small aircraft. The airfield appeared to be small, the tower almost insignificant. He was tossed in the back of the aircraft with a collection of duffel bags and as sensation started to fade, he heard two engines cough to life and run up to takeoff speed.

That was all he remembered.

The sun was bright in his face. He was in a room, bound to a chair, the sun streaming through the windows that were covered only by sheers, a gauzy material that was useless against the sun.

His mouth was dry from the drugs. He had no idea how long he had been out. They had taken him with just six days to go. He wondered how many were left.

Carter was able to move his head freely, though the more he moved the more his head throbbed. He bent his head and rubbed his beard against the shoulder of his shirt. The stubble felt like no more than a day's growth of beard.

The door opened and three men came in. Two held submachine guns. They were Kalashnikovs of Finnish manufacture. Trust the KGB to stick to guns they knew, Carter thought. The third man was short and fat, his three chins competing with each other for space between his jawbone and chest. He was without hair, a domed butterball with the pink complexion typical of the dedicated gourmand.

"You are feeling better, Commander Carlson?" the fat man asked in French.

"I've felt better."

"Your French is excellent. It pains me to detain you this way. But you should not try to be what you are not, Commander. It will get you in trouble every time."

The fat man seemed to have all the time in the world. Carter knew who he was but wasn't about to reveal that information. Jean Sprague had described in detail all the players he hadn't met. This one was Serge Savarin, second only to the new leader of the separatists. That fact, plus the ride in the twin-engine plane, confirmed that he was somewhere in Québec. Savarin could not afford to be far from the seat of government. Carter had studied maps of the city. The commercial airport was in Ste. Foy. He'd bet that they were within a few miles of the airport.

"I'm not sure what you are getting at. Who the hell are you?"

"That, *mon ami,* is not the question. You are the

question mark and we intend to find you just who you are."

"You're in big trouble, whoever you are. I'm a citizen of the United States. I have diplomatic immunity."

"A joke," the fat man laughed, his belly almost shaking him off balance. Then he recovered, his face set grimly. "My friends are skilled at making people talk. They are crude fellows, not like the men in white coats and soft hands from Serbsky."

So Savarin knew about the Serbsky Institute, the Soviet's notorious training school for interrogation specialists. That fact alone condemned him. He knew too much to be a recent convert. The statement was also good news in a way. Carter dreaded only one thing that the Soviets could do to him under interrogation: they could fry his brain with drugs they had developed that went beyond the Geneva Convention's rules. More than one AXE agent had been rescued only to spend the rest of his or her life as a vegetable. He could take any kind of physical torture they could dish out, but the thought of drugs developed at Serbsky almost gave him nightmares.

Savarin left the room and the two big men went to work.

"Get the hand generator, Yuri," one said, assuming Carter couldn't understand Russian.

The one called Yuri left the room for a few seconds while the other untied Carter. He didn't allow the man from AXE enough freedom of movement to do any damage before his partner returned.

"The wires are all tangled, Gregor. It will take time."

"Damn! I will do it. Take off his pants."

The one called Gregor held the Kalashnikov in the

crook of one arm while he untangled the wires that looked like a group of electrodes with alligator clips at each end.

Carter steeled himself for a painful session. It was reassuring to know that he'd endured torture like this before without being broken, but unnerving to know in advance the excruciating effect of electrical currents run through the most sensitive parts of the body.

"Pull up his shirt," Gregor ordered, clamping alligator clips to the terminals of the generator.

Carter had been retied so that his feet were secured to the legs of the chair and his arms around the sides. He was naked except for a shirt pulled up to his chin and a pair of socks.

Gregor approached, a wicked grin on his face. "This may sting a little, Amerikanski," he said in heavily accented English as he clipped one terminal to Carter's left breast and the other to the skin of his scrotum.

"Turn the rotor, Yuri," Gregor said. "Take the needle to fifty volts only."

Carter was surprised that they were using a hand-cranked generator. It seemed crude.

The big Soviet agent turned the handle but nothing happened. When he came up to the speed he wanted, he flipped a switch.

The current shocked Carter, even at the low voltage. He stiffened as searing pain coursed through his abdominal muscles from his nipple to his crotch. The muscles went into spasm. Long after Yuri stopped cranking, the pain persisted as the muscles knotted.

Gregor nodded to his partner. "One hundred."

Yuri cranked faster. The pain reached out beyond the

cramped muscles to explode in every nerve ending of his body. He looked through watery eyes, almost expecting to see flames shooting from his skin, but it was all sensation. It was as if a torch had been thrust into his crotch and another into his chest.

The bonds kept him from straightening like a board. The raw hemp chewed into his skin everywhere it touched, as his body fought the current.

"Enough, Yuri. We will be patient and wait for our friend to tell us what we want to know."

"Go to hell!" Carter ground out through his teeth. Even his jaw ached from grinding upper and lower together. During the worst of it, he had bitten through the inside of his cheek and blood ran from the corner of his mouth.

"Who are you, Commander Carlson? Your real name, please, and the organization you work for," Gregor asked with obscene politeness as he adjusted the clips on either side of Carter's scrotum. "I'm waiting," he said when Carter was silent.

"Go to hell," Carter muttered again, preparing himself for what was to come.

Yuri didn't wait for a command. He cranked the handle furiously.

Carter saw the needle pass 200, then all he saw was white light. Every nerve in his body screamed out as the pain ripped through every cell starting at his crotch. It threatened to blow the top off his head as he felt the pressure build.

Then everything went black as if someone had thrown a light switch. The last thought Carter had was of life and

death. At times like these he never knew whether he
would awake.

"You have the commander?"

"Yes. He's with two of our men."

"What has he told you?"

"Not a thing yet. But he will."

"What do you mean, you weak-kneed bastard?" the
voice of control asked. "He's not some kind of super-
man. I want to know everything he can tell you in the
next hour. I'll be waiting."

"But . . . he's unconscious now. He's stronger than
anyone we've ever encountered. It . . . it's going to
take time."

"You're a disgrace to the party, Savarin. All right. It's
nine o'clock. Call me at midnight."

Carter opened one eye and, with pain searing his
eyeball, he opened the other. The room was dark except
for one bare bulb over his head. Every muscle was sore
from the spasms that had passed through his body. The
muscles of his abdomen were no longer knotted, but
they, along with his testicles, bore the brunt of the pain.

He moved carefully. Pain wracked his tortured body,
but he had to move. The rope at one wrist was so tight he
couldn't feel his hand at all, but the other had some play.
It had been loosened by the gyrations he'd been through
as the current surged through him.

He tried to wiggle the wrist free. It wouldn't come. He
tried harder. The rope slipped partway off his wrist, but
the effort cost him the battle. He passed out again.

When he came to again, he didn't know how much

time had passed. Nothing had changed in the room. But his one hand was still free.

He couldn't free the other wrist. He bent over with difficulty, his groin screaming with the effort. He reached the rope of one ankle. It took him at least fifteen minutes to free it. The other ankle took longer. He worried about the time it was taking, but he couldn't do any better.

Slowly he was able to swivel around so that his free hand was working on the rope around his left wrist.

He heard footsteps while he was still working on the impossibly tight knots, The door handled turned. Yuri stood inside the door, his Kalashnikov slung over his shoulder, a stunned look on his face.

With every bit of strength he had left, Carter spun around, his left hand still secured to the chair. The seat caught the Soviet agent under the chin and lifted him off his feet. Carter fell to the floor, part of the splintered chair still attached to his left hand.

He heard feet pounding up stairs not far from the door. With every muscle in his body crying out in pain, he pulled the gun from the Russian's shoulder. He was still on the floor, fumbling with the gun, when the door burst open and Gregor stood over him.

The safety was finally off. He shifted the gun, holding the trigger guard in his right hand, the stock against his right leg, then squeezed.

The gun sprayed 7.62mm steel-capped missiles to the far side of the room at the rate of more than seven hundred a minute. Gregor was thrown back against the door, his body stitched with bullets. The gun continued to roar in Carter's weakened hand until the banana clip was empty.

The Killmaster tried to sit up, to defend himself against any possible attack, and looked to see what had happened to Yuri.

Gregor had slid down, against the door, painting the faded wood with his blood. His companion lay on the floor, blood oozing from his nose, mouth, and ears. Carter figured he must have shattered his skull when he hit the floor. He looked at Carter as his eyes glazed. His mouth started to work, but no words came out as his head slowly fell to one side.

Carter gained strength from the sight. He was able to sit up and go to work on his wrist. When he was free, he crawled to the door and felt for a pulse. Gregor was dead. To his surprise, Yuri's heart still beat faintly.

Carter sat with his mouth next to the dying man's ear. "Yuri. Yuri. It is your last moment. Time to confess," he said in Russian.

The bloodied mouth tried to move but nothing came out.

Carter moved closer. He strained to hear if the breath that was expelled was a last confession.

"Hunger . . ."

"Say it one more time," Carter urged.

"Hung . . . ary . . ."

Carter felt for a pulse again and found none.

In the mesh-enclosed room that was Loomis's office, the regular features of the tall CIA station chief were twisted as he raged at Brown. The black man sat, his face a mask of hate.

"Where the hell is he? What the hell's he doing?" Loomis barked.

"I don't know. He disappeared yesterday."

"I blame the schoolyard fiasco on him. That bastard's doing exactly what I specifically ordered him not to do. He's making waves all over the damned place."

"But he's at least getting some results. We know the men in the car were foreign agents," Brown countered.

"We're not sure of that. We don't know who they're tied in with. Shit!"

"We're farther ahead than before he arrived," Brown reminded him.

"And you've been working with that slippery bastard," Loomis accused. "I told you to keep an eye on him, not help him."

"I haven't helped him directly," Brown lied. "Can I pull off the surveillance now?"

"No. I want them covering Sprague's apartment, the prime minister's house, and his damned hotel."

"I think it's a waste of time."

"I don't give a damn what you think! And you know what that brings up? It seriously compromises your performance review. You won't work in a decent station in the Company if you don't shape up."

"Is that all?"

"Isn't that enough? Now get the hell out of here and find Carlson and bring him back here!"

Brown moved from the chair, happy to be dismissed.

"Tell Sprague I want to see her," Loomis shouted at Brown's back.

Jean was walking down the corridor when she heard

her name. She knocked on Loomis's door. "Did I hear my name mentioned?"

"What the hell are you doing at my door?"

She looked startled. "I was just passing."

"Sit down and tell me what you know about this Carlson," he growled at her. His face, normally a picture of confidence and authority, was suffused with a light crimson flush.

"Why?"

"What the hell do you . . . ? Because I ordered you to, that's why!"

"I don't work for you, Loomis. You can't bark at me like the others," she said, getting to her feet.

"Where is he? What's he doing," Loomis asked, calmer.

"I don't know."

"You've spent some time with him. What did he tell you?"

"Listen, Loomis, what he does and what he may or may not tell me is the business of the ambassador and our superior officers. You want answers, call Niles," she said as she stormed out.

In the corridor away from Loomis's office, Brown stopped her and handed her a fresh mug of coffee. "Don't let him get to you," he said.

"I can handle myself."

"I heard. I envy you."

She sensed a hesitation in him. "Do you want something, Frank?"

"You've gotten close to Carlson. So have I. He seems to trust both of us and he's got Loomis pegged all the way."

"So?"

"I'm worried about him. He's dropped out of sight."

"My God! You don't think . . ."

"He's either on to something he couldn't tell us about, or they've got him."

They walked back to her small office and closed the door. He turned on a small radio and sought the static between stations. He motioned her to stand with him. "I think this is a lot bigger than Loomis suspects. I think Carlson is a lot more than he wants us to believe."

"So why tell me?"

"He trusts me. We're working together. I think he trusts you. If he calls you, I want you to give him a number he can get me at day or night."

"And can I trust you, Frank, or are you another Loomis, a man out for your own glory?"

"If you haven't figured that out yet, Jean, then we're wasting each other's time."

She smiled at him and whispered over the static. "I'll tell him. What's the number?"

Carter found strength enough to pull on his scattered clothing and push Gregor's blood-covered body away from the door. He went back and searched through their pockets for identification. He found none, but he didn't need any more proof that they were KGB or that Savarin was one of them. If Savarin was a foreign agent, did that make Lafontaine one of them? What he needed was proof to show someone else, enough to convict Lafontaine or Savarin, certainly to discredit the separatists before the election. Right now it was just his word against that of the powerful politicians.

He looked around. The rest of the house was a shambles. It was a two-story frame house set off by itself in a rural setting. The bedrooms were filled with discarded clothing, the beds' mattresses on the floor. The kitchen was littered with half-eaten meals. Ants and cockroaches outnumbered the human occupants by thousands to one.

In the room set aside for television and reading, Carter found his weapons and watch in the drawer of an old dresser. He also found several sets of car keys and a pile of small-denomination Canadian bills. With a feeling of confidence he'd not experienced for many hours, he reclaimed his possessions, and walked to the door feeling more like a whole person.

The yard was overgrown with weeds. No vehicles were in sight. He found an old lean-to closed to the elements by two wooden doors on rusted hinges. When he opened them, they creaked loudly in the still night. The musty smell that hit him told of dampness present for many years.

An old Jeep Commando sat on the dirt floor, covered with dust. He tried all the keys until he found one that fitted, knowing he'd be damned lucky if the motor turned over. Sure enough, the motor protested weakly, wheezed, coughed, and died.

He waited a moment and tried it again. It moved less sluggishly, turned over sporadically, then with one loud cough, it caught and started to even out.

Carter backed out of the old shed and headed down a long, dusty lane. A quarter-mile ride took him to a country road, the old Jeep coughing and backfiring all the way.

Left or right? The odds were about even. He scanned the sky for some pollution. It seemed less clear to the right so he headed into the sun, the fading evening sun. It must be the end of the fifth to the last day.

He kept track of the mileage, and came to a small town after sixteen kilometers, almost exactly ten miles. The general store had an ancient telephone booth next to the cracked cement steps out front.

He dialed Jean's number in Ottawa.

"Where are you?" she asked.

"Are you sure your phone's clean?"

"No."

"I'll have to chance it. Do you have a number for Frank Brown?"

"Are you all right?"

"I am now. Can you get his number for me?"

She gave it to him. "Where are you, Nick?" she asked again.

"I'm not exactly sure, but I'll be back in Ottawa tonight. I'll be in touch."

He hung up and dialed Brown's number. The two calls took all the quarters he was able to get from the taciturn old storekeeper.

"Yes?"

"It's me. Jean gave me the number."

"Good. It's the only clean one here. A buddy and I monitor it," Brown explained. "Where the hell are you?"

"The storekeeper tells me it's just a crossroads two miles west of St-Augustine-De-Québec," he replied.

"Just a minute. I've got a map," he said. He was gone

for no more than ten seconds. "I've got it. That's just east of the Ste. Foy airport."

"I thought so. How are we going to play this? I have to get back there fast."

"I'll call Saunders. He's got a close friend in the Québec Provincial Police. They'll probably pick you up by helicopter."

"Good. One more thing. They held me at a farmhouse. It's exactly ten miles east of the general store where they'll find me."

"They need body bags?"

"A couple. Lafontaine's right-hand man, Serge Savarin, was there, but he didn't stick around."

Brown whistled. "You got anything to tie Lafontaine to them?"

"Not yet, but he's on the top of my list now."

"We'll work on it. In the meantime, hold tight. When you hear a helicopter, move off to a flat area away from the store. They'll be QPP officers. They'll take you to,"—he consulted the map—"a place called Vanleek Hill. We'll be waiting for you."

"Thanks. I appreciate the service. Just five days to the referendum, right?"

"Nope. Four."

EIGHT

Brown and Saunders left him in a safe house the OPP chief had set up for his own CID. It was north of Ottawa in Gatineau Park. The communication was by radio. They left an old Land-Rover for him in case he had to get out fast.

AXE's international computer communications network picked up his signal. He gave the electronic voice his codes and the codes for Hawk's private number.

"Nick," Hawk came on. He seemed out of breath. "How's it going?"

Carter filled him in on recent events, including his problems with Loomis.

"Yeah, I'd heard that he was a hardass. Just a minute. Howard's with me. He might as well hear this first-hand," the crusty old chief of AXE said, pressing the button for loudspeaker broadcast of the call.

Howard Schmidt handled Records at AXE headquarters. He was also the gadgets specialist and the weapons expert. As if that wasn't enough, he was also in charge of Recognitions. A longtime friend and confidant of

Carter's, the only time Schmidt's company wasn't welcome was when he sat Carter down for a session on personnel, noting the changes to agents on the other side.

"Good. Howard can help on this one."

"Shoot," Schmidt said.

"Two KGB musclemen were working for Serge Savarin outside of Québec City."

"The name rings a bell, but run him by me again," Hawk said.

"He's Lafontaine's right-hand man. That means Lafontaine could be the brains behind the Parisant killing or Savarin is pulling the strings," Carter suggested. "Do you have anything on him, Howard?"

"Small potatoes. He was identified as a Communist sympathizer years ago, but he's been clean since."

"What do you think, sir?" Carter asked his boss.

"You're on the scene, Nick. It's your baby. Savarin complicates the issue. We can't assume Lafontaine is involved directly."

"Looks that way. But I've got a feeling we've got something deeper here," Carter said. "Lafontaine's too obvious, and I don't think he's too bright."

"What are you getting at?" Hawk asked.

"Someone else is pulling his strings."

"Someone from Moscow?" Schmidt asked.

"No. Someone here—someone with power—someone with some kind of master plan."

"I'll go along with that," Hawk said. "Your hunches usually pay off. Follow them."

Carter told them about the last word of the dying Soviet agent. "It sounded like *Hungary*. But I don't get the connection."

"Unless they've got a deep plant that came in from Hungary," Hawk mused.

"Something in my files could help," Schmidt suggested. "I remember hearing about a plot about the time of the Hungarian uprising. The Soviets were to plant a mole in Ottawa at an early age—a young kid—and bring him along under cover in Canada," Schmidt went on. "It didn't prove out way back then, and just surfaced when one of their agents defected a few years back."

"The timing fits," Carter said. "But who could it be?"

"The defector told us a ten-year-old boy was brought in by a Hungarian couple during a large influx of refugees in 1956," Schmidt said. "It was a confusing time."

"You should pull the file and give Nick the rest right away," Hawk said. "We've got only four days."

"Will do," Schmidt said. "But more is coming back to me. The defector said the first couple taking care of the boy were to be killed in a car accident."

"Bloodthirsty bastards," Hawk muttered. "After all this time I still can't get used to their methods."

"He was taken as a foster child by a second couple," Schmidt continued. "After they were drowned in a boating accident, we learned that the accident was a hoax and they'd been deep plants there for years."

"So where's the boy?" Hawk asked.

"The story was all after-the-fact to us," Schmidt explained. "He was legally adopted by a third couple. The records of the adoption agency that suposedly placed him were lost in a fire in 1960."

"That's it?" Carter asked. "You don't have anything tangible? A picture? Fingerprints? Anything?"

"I'll pull the file, but you've heard everything I've got."

Carter knew Schmidt's memory well enough to believe him. "Damn!" he said. "You've just confirmed how important this man is. Have you ever heard of them protecting someone with three layers, three families?"

"No. It's a first for me," Hawk admitted.

And if it was a first for Hawk, it was probably a first, Carter thought. "They had to kill the first family. They were too close to the source—very expendable," the Killmaster said, as if thinking aloud. "The second family was probably recalled and reassigned. They could be anywhere. And the third couple? Who knows? They could still be working deep cover here if they're alive."

"This isn't getting us anywhere," Hawk grumbled. "How are you, Nick?" His tone more solicitous. "Were you badly hurt at all when they took you?"

That was a question Carter never answered directly. "I'm still in action," he said.

"Call if you need anything," Schmidt said.

"Everything's intact, Howard," he said as he switched off.

One hell of a mess, he thought to himself. What was the possibility that something could have surfaced here in Canada at the time? After all, they were closer to the action than his friends in Washington.

There were too many unanswered questions, he reflected. How had the separatists managed to go so far, and why now?

He picked up the transmit key and flipped on the set again. He turned to a frequency Brown had given him.

"Can you get both Tanks and Saunders for a brainstorming session?" he asked. "I've come up with something new that could help."

"I'll try. Don't leave the cabin for a couple of hours. I'll get back to you."

Brown had supplied Carter with a bottle of Chivas Regal, and Carter had been nursing it over the past few hours. He sat for a long time recalling every scrap of information he had on the case, deciding on his next move. He couldn't count on the chief of the Ottawa police or the head of the Ontario Provincial Police to come up with something concrete. He'd have to get it for himself.

All he had was Savarin, or possibly Lafontaine. He also knew he had only three days. Carter was sure the man would feel secure if the referendum went his way. Québec would then become a free entity. He could probably sew up the QPP, effectively his own military, and he'd be a dictator. He or Lafontaine. No one could touch him after that—not legally.

Time passed slowly. While he was thinking, a light on the radio blinked, its red light flashing.

"Yes?" he answered cautiously.

"Frank asked me to call. He was able to pick up both Tanks and Saunders. They should almost be there by now."

"Who is this?"

"Frank told you only one other man uses this radio. That's me. You don't have to know who I am."

Carter switched off. The man was right, and he was smart. He began to plan his questions.

He had just finished organizing his thoughts, when he heard tires on gravel. He slipped his Luger from beneath his left arm and sneaked out the back door. He watched as a black GM Jimmy came to a stop and the three men he'd been expecting climbed from the car. He walked around to the front, returning the gun to its holster.

The big man with the crew cut and massive belly smiled at the sight of the gun. "You expecting some varmints, pardner?" Chief Tanks joked. The second man stared at the disappearing gun through his black-rimmed glasses.

Brown followed them up to the cabin and closed the door. Carter offered them scotch and had no refusals.

"I've been talking to my people," he started. "They've come up with an interesting hypothesis." He told them what he'd learned from Howard Schmidt.

"Interesting," Saunders mused, stroking his chin. "I've heard the story too."

"Where?" Carter asked immediately.

"A friend with the RCMP saw a file. A good friend. A woman with total clearance."

"Who shall remain nameless," Tanks said, laughing. A great deal of what Tanks said was punctuated with a laugh.

"But who has control of the archives? Exactly what do we need?" Brown asked.

"Pictures," Carter said.

"But the kid was maybe ten or eleven at the most. He'd be in his middle forties now," Brown noted.

"And that in itself narrows the field," Carter said.

"We've got little time for speculation," Tanks added.

"All right. Anything you can get. But particularly pictures," Carter said. "I've decided to go after Savarin and Lafontaine."

"Alone?" Brown asked.

"I work best that way."

"There's something you ought to know," Brown went on, his face a mask, his emotions hidden. "We can't locate Jean Sprague. She's just dropped out of the picture."

Carter felt the shock grab at his gut. "Any ideas?" he asked.

"Two men were seen with her near her place. We didn't get the licence number," Tanks offered, his tone subdued.

"I've got three addresses for Lafontaine. One seems promising," Brown offered.

"Did Loomis have anything to do with her disappearance?" Carter asked.

"What the hell kind of a question is that?" Tanks asked.

"Look. I have to eliminate all possibilities," Carter explained. "Loomis could be pumping her. She hasn't been gone very long."

"I'd say no on that score," Brown said. "First, I've had men on Loomis since you became the man of the hour. Second, he's got too much at stake to blow it on such a stupid move."

"Let's hope he thinks that way," Carter growled.

"Well, what do you need?" Brown asked.

"One helicopter painted black and someone I can trust to fly it."

"That'll be my pleasure," Saunders said. "I'll have someone on it in a minute," he said, reaching for a telephone.

"Don't forget the file on the mole," Carter reminded

him. "The sooner we get a look at that RCMP file the better."

"One last thing," Tanks said, holding his hand over Saunders's hand on the phone. "We keep Turner and Hume out of it. If we're dealing with a mole, let's keep it to the people in this room."

"Agreed," Carter said. "But hold off on the helicopter. I've just had another idea. Is it possible to get clearance from all services and your Department of Transport radar people?"

"No problem," Saunders said. "I give you a special OPP code and radio frequency. I'll cover it with Québec if you want."

"I want."

"It's done. What do you have in mind?"

"I might have my own vehicle. What if I wanted it brought in by C-31 transport from Washington?"

"No problem," Saunders said. "When?"

"Tonight."

Carter coded in his identification to the AXE computer again. "Get me Howard Schmidt even if you have to drag him out of the shower." He didn't wait long.

"Nick? That you again?"

"Yeah, Howard. And I'm short on time. They've taken Jean Sprague."

"The G-2 woman at the embassy?"

"The same. I've got to get to her fast. How's the secret chopper you've been working on?"

"Strange you should ask. We test-flew her today."

"I want her here as fast as you can manage. I've got clearance for a C-31 flight into Ottawa tonight."

"You've got it."

"And Howard, I want her to be flat black."

"We'll paint her in flight. The C-31's big enough. No problem."

"Did you perfect the silent mode?"

"You can't hear her from fifty feet away when you use the silent mode. But you've got to get her down below fifty knots to make it work."

"No problem. What about payload? Can I take a passenger?"

"Now, that could be a problem. She's a one-man plane and loaded with weaponry. Unless you want me to strip her . . ."

"I want all the firepower I can get."

"I could take off two rocket pods. How big is the passenger?"

"One-twenty."

"You've got it."

"Stick some C-4 plastique and timers in the chopper. Better include a couple of lethal Pierres."

"That it?"

"Isn't that enough? I could conduct a one-man war with that load."

"And if I know you, that's exactly what you'll be doing."

Saunders had supplied the precise locations of Lafontaine's three main strongholds in Québec. The old Lafontaine estate was located across the road from the College of Jesuits on Boulevard Ste. Cyrille. It was as old as the college, built of gray granite and almost as old as the Jesuit sanctuary. The outer fringes of the city had long since surrounded it.

The second location supplied by Saunders and his QPP friends was a farm outside of the town of St. Adolphe, no more than twenty miles northeast of the city. The third location was within the boundary of a provincial park almost sixty miles directly north of the city. Saunders's contacts described it as an old ranger station that Lafontaine had bought for a song when a new building was built for the park rangers.

Carter was flying between Trois-Rivières and Québec City checking out Schmidt's new toy. It had originally been a Bell 680-LHX that was revolutionary in its capability for silent flight even before Schmidt got his hands on it. All weapons systems contracted into compartments within the body. From a distance it didn't look any different than a traffic helicopter from a local TV station up for a routine perusal of the major highways.

The firepower was awesome, although Carter didn't expect to use what he had. With two missile launchers removed to accommodate another passenger, he still had six Penguin air-to-ship missiles and two pods of rotary 60mm cannon. In a compartment directly beneath his feet he had a cluster bomb that would glide to within a couple of hundred feet of the ground before releasing fifty smaller bombs that could decimate a regiment.

Carter was not a soldier. He was not on a seek-and-destroy mission. His job was to uncover the mole, discredit him, and preserve the continuity of government for his country's best neighbor. But first, he had to find Jean and make sure she was out of danger.

He was dressed as he had been on his earlier sorties.

He still had the black fatigues. Wilhelmina, his 9mm Luger, and Hugo, a pencil-thin stiletto, were strapped in place, in plain view. The only personal weapons not in evidence were the pair of miniaturized gas bombs he wore, one strapped to each inner thigh. Many years earlier, he'd dubbed the type of bomb "Pierre." He usually carried only one, but he had a hunch one would not suffice on this trip.

Québec City came at him sooner than he expected. No one had challenged him. Obviously Saunders had done his job well. The Bell 680 was equipped with electronic monitors and a computer to display every square mile of North American territory in a grid pattern. Carter looked up the grid coordinates for Québec, and the city was spread out for him on a dull green screen.

An arrow traced his flight along the electronic map. He followed Chemin Ste. Foy and cut across to the College of Jesuits at Monk Avenue. Carter went into silent mode, then switched on another monitor that showed him the landscape immediately below. The old Lafontaine homestead was well outlined.

He circled for a better visual sighting. The place looked deserted. He switched on the infrared heat sensors and viewed a third monitor. Four people were evident, two on the grounds and two in the house. The two on the grounds were patrolling. One in the house was in the kitchen; one was in a bedroom obviously asleep, probably Mrs. Lafontaine.

Carter decided that he would be wasting his time at the city house. It was poorly located to be the center of activity for a big subversive operation. He turned to port, switched to full power, and headed for the farm.

The farm was miles from any other farm to the north of St. Adolphe. His heat sensors told him that ten people occupied the house and grounds. Carter knew he'd have to go down. Howard Schmidt's equipment was state of the art, but it couldn't tell him if Jean Sprague was one of those ten.

In silent mode he made a visual sighting of the farmhouse. It was surrounded by a high fence with what looked like barbed wire on the top. The inside of the perimeter was too small for him to land undetected, so he picked a clearing about a mile away and headed for the house on foot.

Looped around one shoulder was a scaling rope and under his arm was the floor covering from the bottom of the chopper. He wore the goggles Schmidt had designed to detect laser surveillance.

The grounds were quiet. His chopper's sensors had told him that three of the sources of body heat were outside the house. He chose the most remote corner of the property he could find and swung the scaling rope to the top of the fence. It caught on the razor-sharp slices of steel that were more deadly than barbed wire.

The chopper's floor mat shielded Carter from the fence as he dropped silently to the ground. Remembering the dogs on Boisvert's property, he was wary. But after ten minutes of waiting he heard nothing that would suggest canine patrols.

The goggles were not detecting surveillance lasers, so Carter pocketed them and headed for the house. Near the back door a huge figure stood stock-still, his eyes surveying the grounds.

Noiselessly, Carter slipped closer. He was next to

invisible with his black clothes and the black greasepaint on his face.

The man's back was to the house. There was no way Carter could get around him.

Carter slipped Hugo to his right palm. He held the blade and flipped the needlelike stiletto on a direct line with the man's heart. With speed that would challenge the best sprinter in the world, Carter caught the body before it hit the ground.

He went through the man's pockets. The most obvious clue to the man's nationality was a Makarov automatic pistol. The second clue was the man's suit. The poorly tailored suit could only have been made in the Soviet Union. He retrieved the stiletto, wiped it clean, and slipped it in its chamois sheath.

The discoveries made things easier for him. If the guard was KGB, this was a KGB hideout all the way.

He opened the door of the farmhouse with caution, his Luger in his hand, a silencer screwed on its barrel.

A man inside saw the door open, saw the silenced Luger, and drew a gun from his waistband. Carter fired before the other man could pull the trigger.

On the ground floor, three men sat playing cards in a back room. They were drinking vodka and shouting out their play in Russian.

Carter slipped inside the room and leveled his gun at them. "Your names and rank, please," he said.

They looked at him as if he were mad, then the oldest of them, the senior man, laughed aloud and went for his gun in a coat nearby.

Carter shot him through the head, spraying the others with blood and brain matter. "Your names and rank, please," he repeated, waving the Luger at them, insisting they remain seated.

No one spoke. Carter sat in the chair deserted by the dead man. He reached into the fold of his fatigues. "The last time," he said. "Your names and rank."

One man was about to speak, but the other chopped him across the throat with the back of his hand.

Carter twisted the two halves of the tiny bomb, took a deep breath, and dropped the lethal orb on the floor.

When the two men slumped where they sat, he went through their pockets. These were not drones. One was a captain from the dreaded First Chief Directorate, a killer. He must have been extremely confident to carry identification.

The other man carried no identification. He had no weapons. His hands were soft. He had the smell of fresh soap and alcohol about him. A doctor perhaps? The first man he shot also carried no ID.

Carter had no more time to speculate. Five down and five to go.

He closed the door on the lethal gas and stood in the hall breathing deeply and listening to the sounds of the house. It was still. He decided to try the bedrooms. He snaked up the steps to the second floor. One after the other he tried the three bedrooms and the bathroom, but found no one.

A narrow stair led to the top floor. Halfway up it he heard what sounded like someone snoring. As he drew nearer, the sound increased and he had no trouble locating the room. As a precaution, he checked the other rooms and found them empty. A couple occupied the last one. That brought the total to seven.

Carefully, he removed Howard Schmidt's drug case from a hip pocket. He filled a syringe with a drug that would knock these two out for an hour or more, and carefully plunged it into the man's arm. Before he could react to the slight prick, the big, raw-boned man was in dreamland once again.

The wife awoke and stared into the barrel of the gun.

"I won't hurt you," Carter said in French.

The woman remained silent. "Do you work with them?" he asked.

"We are simple farmers, monsieur. They are worse than animals."

"This will not hurt you. Don't worry." Before she knew what was happening, Carter had injected the syringe and she was asleep in seconds.

Carter returned to the ground floor and looked for an entrance to a basement. Suddenly he heard a very faint voice; it seemed to be coming from a floor below. He found a basement door and charged down, his gun in hand. A frightened man was bleating into the mike of a long-range radio.

". . . I found two of them dead. Something's—"

Carter put a 9mm slug through his head and turned off the set. Before he could react to a noise behind him, he felt something rip through the muscle of his left arm, then heard the bark of a gun.

The blast turned him to face the snarling features of a small man holding a gun that seemed like a cannon in his small hand. Carter fired before the man could get off another shot.

That made nine. Carter slipped into a dark corner and

tied a handkerchief around the wounded arm before he went on.

The cellar smelled like a cross between a locker room and a barn. He peeked around the corner from his hiding place. He saw no one but the two dead men.

He crouched down and sat for a full five minutes, listening.

Nothing.

Then, faintly at first, he heard moaning, and a scraping sound from a room nearby.

Cautiously he crept nearer to the sound. He opened the door a crack and peered inside. A man lay on a cot. Carter opened the door wider and went in, covering the man with his gun. He must have presented an awesome sight to the man cringed against the wall for he moaned louder.

The man, obviously a prisoner, was very slim. His clothes seemed to hang on him, jutting out at his shoulders. The man's nose was his strongest feature.

"Mr. Lafontaine. What are you doing here?"

"Who are you?" the gaunt, unshaven face asked.

"Commander Nicholas Carlson. We met at the American embassy a few days ago."

"Impossible. I've been here . . . I don't know . . . a long time. I don't know you . . ."

"You've nothing to fear from me. I'll take you out. Can you walk?"

"I think so."

Carter helped him up the cellar stairs and led him out the front door. He left the scaling rope and took the weakened man through a back gate. He practically had to carry him the last few hundred yards.

The helicopter stood ready.

"Do you know where the chief of the provincial police lives?"

"Of course."

"Good. I want you in his house until this is over. I don't want anyone to know you're alive."

"Why, for heaven's sake?"

"It's a long story, Mr. Lafontaine," Carter explained in French. "Someone is taking your place. Impersonating you. Someone very dangerous to your country."

"Will you have Jacques Carreau call me?"

"I promise, but it might be a few hours. Will you sit tight until you hear?"

"I don't feel up to much else."

"Good. I've got something else to do first."

"Who are you? Who do you work for?"

"I'm with the prime minister's special staff," Carter lied. He didn't have time for explanations. Time was very short.

NINE

Alone in the chopper, Carter felt he was back on track.
Physically, his arm ached a bit, but otherwise he felt
pretty good. At the moment he had the advantage. He
had the helicopter and they didn't know he was on their
trail. Savarin would have tipped his people off, but they
didn't know he was on the way to Lac Gregory.

With uncanny accuracy, the grid map monitor told him
where the lodge was located. He circled the lodge, a
rather small log building on the south shore of the lake,
without seeing any sign of life. It was daybreak and the
days were draining away all too fast.

He turned on the heat sensor and scanned the monitor
at an altitude of a hundred feet. The chopper was in silent
mode.

It didn't make sense to him. The sensors picked out
too many heat sources that were human bodies. Some
came in sharply as if in the lodge. Others were less
sharp, as if on another level. Some bodies seemed to
give off faint images as if they were some distance away,
deeper, in some kind of lower basement.

107

The most puzzling images were those not located within the confines of the lodge itself, or below it. Some seemed to be some distance from the lodge. Perhaps there was a cavern, Carter figured. They had either connected the basement to a natural cavern or carved one out. Whatever it was, it existed and had to be investigated. And was that where they had taken Jean? If the answer to that was yes, the next question was how to get her without running into every guard they had. It looked as if there were at least twenty people down there. He decided to make another swing over the lodge before going in.

He studied the heat sensor monitor until his eyes were bleary from the green images. The bodies seemed to be on three levels. Everyone moved at one time or another while he watched, except one. It was in a room on the second level, probably a basement. They seemed to leave that one alone. Maybe they had too much to do before the referendum. Maybe it wasn't Jean, just someone like Serge Savarin who had work to do at a desk.

Enough speculation. He had to go in.

"You're telling me you had him under control and he's escaped?"

"I don't know how he did it. Yuri and Gregor are dead. What the hell will I do now?"

"What indeed? He knows who you are and your connection to us."

"But he might not have told anyone."

"Don't be naïve. It seems to me that this one is too

professional not to keep his people informed. Where are you now?"

"At the lodge."

"Keep everything running smoothly. Don't leave the lodge. I'll try to get more help there as soon as I can."

"I don't like the fact that he knows about me," Savarin whined.

"Nor do I, Serge. Nor do I. If we were home, you would be on a one-way trip to a very cold climate."

"It's still going to work. Believe me. Two more days and no one can stop us."

"You'd better keep on thinking that, Serge. You'd better make it work."

Carter set the chopper down a few hundred yards from the lodge. He had memorized everything he'd seen on the monitors and he was as well equipped as the wizardry of Howard Schmidt could make him. The laser-sensor goggles were in place. The rucksack full of plastique was no more than a slight burden. His favorite weapons were snug in their usual places. In the early mist of morning he looked like something black and ominous from outer space.

No one was outdoors. Carter soon learned the reason. A pattern of laser beams crisscrossed the ground for fifty feet from the old, moss-covered log building.

It was too light for cover. The beams were too close for a headlong rush to the house. Some were too high to climb over. Some were too close together to allow him to crawl beneath with the rucksack on his back.

At one point he felt like going back to the chopper and unloading all six missiles on the lodge and then examining the remains. But he had two good reasons why that would be a bad move. One was the probability that Jean was in the building. The other was a natural curiosity. This could be their headquarters. He had to see what they were hiding there.

It was dangerous, but he unstrapped the rucksack and started across the labyrinth of beams. It took him a good half hour, and when he'd finally made it, he was soaked with sweat. He had crawled on his belly, slipped bent half double between some beams, and hurdled others with inches to spare. It was a miracle that no one had seen him from the lodge.

He stopped near the front door to collect his thoughts. No surveillance cameras were in sight. Whoever was inside must have extreme confidence in the laser beams.

The lone body he had seen in the monitor was at the back and one level below the ground. Somehow, he'd have to get there first.

Hundreds of miles away in Ottawa, Robert Boisvert sat in Prime Minister Carreau's office going through some papers he had to sign as deputy prime minister. Carreau's secretary had left them before she'd gone home late the night before. They had to be ready for the morning session. Thoughts of Marie Carreau kept interfering with his work. The affair had been exciting at first—the delicious risk of taking her almost under the eyes of the SSS, the newness of her as a lover, the information she had supplied that had moved his plans ahead much faster.

Unlike Carreau, Boisvert was not an early riser. It was not unusual to see Carreau arrive to start the business of the day at six, but that was not for his deputy. Eight was a better time for Boisvert, or even nine. The bell to call members into session never rang before ten and he always had time, at least an hour, to prepare for what usually turned out to be a boring day.

But this was different. Carreau was making a swing through the western provinces to shore up party confidence. Boisvert ought to know: he was with Marie in the prime minister's bed the night before.

He was thinking about her foolishness, her stubborn desire for them to divorce their spouses, when he thought he heard a commotion in the hall. Marie would not venture out of the Sussex Drive residence for their dalliance. He'd tried often enough to get her to try a hotel or even a rented apartment, but they were both so recognizable, and she had to deal with her SSS guard. It always seemed strange cuckolding the most powerful man in the country in his own bed.

The commotion outside grew louder, then suddenly, the door flew open and two hooded men burst in, each with an automatic pistol in his hand.

He felt as if a horse had kicked him in the shoulder, and he went down behind the desk. The firing continued, spraying the room over his head with what seemed like hundreds of rounds. He felt a sharp pain in his foot and pulled it, bleeding, behind the desk with him.

Other shots were fired, not the steady rhythm of the small-caliber pistols, but the sharp bark of individual shots from larger guns.

Finally all was still. A security man was crouching over him.

"Are you all right, Mr. Boisvert?"

"My shoulder . . . one of my feet," the deputy prime minister managed before he passed out.

The paramedics and the house doctor were there in seconds. Boisvert regained consciousness as they placed him on a stretcher, an intravenous tube in his right arm. As he was carried from the office, he saw the two gunmen in their own pools of blood near the door. Down the hall, blankets covered three bodies that he assumed to be SSS men assigned to protect him.

"Call my wife," he whispered to the physician, a man he'd known for years. "And keep Mrs. Carreau away from the hospital."

The doctor, an old hand at Parliament Hill, understood and couldn't agree more.

Carter found that few of the lasers had their origin on the walls of the house. A pathway two feet wide allowed him to roam. He made his way to the back of the old structure easily. Against the back wall, a cellar door, the kind made of wood that folded out and up like two barn doors, was the only way in. They were covered with wet leaves that had obviously fallen the winter before.

Hugo slipped between them, giving Carter a purchase to pull. One rose ponderously, making enough noise to wake the dead.

Carter slipped inside and was immediately accosted by a huge guard with a Kalashnikov cocked and ready. Carter was lucky: the guard was like a robot and had no orders to fire inside the house. The big man's hesitation gained him a vicious karate chop to the neck that would keep him out of action for a few minutes.

Next to the guard, a door was closed. Carter opened it and breathed a sigh of relief. Jean was in her bra and panties, tied to a bed, her feet attached to the foot of the bed, her wrists tied by short lengths of rope to the bed posts above her head.

"Are you all right?" he whispered. "Did they drug you?"

"No," said, shaking her head. "I'm stiff, but I'm okay."

"I'll cut you loose in a minute."

He hoisted the guard and brought him inside. Then Hugo went to work on Jean's bonds. When she was free, he slung the guard on the bed while she hunted for the rest of her clothes.

The red vial was the one he sought. Pentothol. It never failed. He plunged the needle in the man's arm and waited for it to take effect.

Jean joined him at the bedside when she was dressed. "What do you intend to do?" she asked. "The place is crawling with types like him."

"They must have something immediate planned or they wouldn't have left you alone. I want to know what it is."

He slapped the man's face softly from side to side. "This is Colonel Popolov, KGB. Your rank and name, quickly," Carter said, using his best Muskovite dialect.

"Boris Spastovski . . . corporal . . . formerly of the . . . Imperial Guard."

"You must have been a bad boy, Boris, to be sent to this outpost."

"What are you asking him?" she said, poking his arm.

He put a hand over her mouth. "I don't want him to hear another voice," he whispered in her ear.

"Why are the others not in here with the woman?" he asked, turning back to the guard.

"They will be here . . . soon. They . . . upstairs . . . meeting room."

"And the others?"

"Guards . . . in the cavern."

"How many?"

"Six. No . . . five. Anatole was taken out sick." He moaned and thrashed about. Carter held him still.

"One more question. Where is the meeting?"

"A colonel . . . you don't know?"

"I've just arrived to take command. Now tell me or you're going under the lash. You've been under the lash, Corporal?"

"Upstairs . . . back of the hall . . . turn right."

Carter switched to the orange syringe and put the man out for hours, then he led Jean up the steps. At the top he turned right and heard the sound of voices. A guard turned from the door and spotted them, but Hugo was out and jutting from the man's jugular before he could act. Blood ran from him, spurting on his chest. Jean moved past Carter, caught the man, and eased him to the ground, the blood pouring over her. Carter pulled the knife from the dead man, wiped it clean, and slipped it back in place. He drew his gun and whispered for Jean to stand back.

With the speed of a leopard, Carter opened the door and stood with the silenced gun covering the group. They had been speaking in French, but the room was silent now as every eye was upon him.

Savarin was at the head of the table, his dome-shaped head shining under the fluorescents above. Carter handed the gun to Jean and walked calmly to the man. He jerked him from his seat and hauled him along the side of the room and tossed him into the hall. Then he told Jean to back up slowly until she was in the hall, never letting the Luger waver.

When she was through the doorway, he tossed his second tiny bomb onto the table in front of the remaining men and slammed the door shut, holding it against the pressure of their attempted escape until he felt no more resistance.

"What did you do to them?" Jean asked.

Carter said nothing, now pointing his gun at Savarin.

"You killed them?"

"As they would have killed us," he growled. "C'mon, Jean, we've got work to do."

Savarin blubbered on the floor at their feet. He was incoherent, begging for his life. Carter hauled him to his feet. "How many guards in here?" he asked.

"Six," Savarin rasped through the spittle running from his mouth.

"That makes five left," Carter said as if to himself. "Now you are going to show us every part of this place, every nook and cranny."

"Shouldn't we get out of here?" Jean whispered. "You've broken their back and there are still four or five guards." ·

"I'd take you back if it were over," he explained. "But we've just met the drones, the ones that make it work. I found the real Guy Lafontaine a prisoner in another of their safe houses. So we have an imposter running loose.

He could be the brains or he could be a pawn. We still don't know."

"I'd still like to get out of here."

"Hang in there, Jean. Something tells me we've just struck gold here. We've got to check it out."

She pulled herself together. "All right. Let's get it over with."

"How are you with weapons?"

"I've had all the courses."

"Good. First we go after the guard's automatic rifle, then we go fishing," Carter said, leading the way down the stairs, pushing the terrified man in front of him as a shield.

Jean picked up the Kalashnikov from the floor of the hall and wiped it clean. She flipped off the safety, chambered a round, and followed Carter down the stairs. "Never mind the other rifle. This one will do."

Carter smiled over his shoulder and led her to the cellar room where he'd found her. A guard was bending over his fallen comrade. Savarin called out. The man turned to be met by a 9mm bullet from Carter's Luger, and went down across the bed.

Jean took the two AK-47s they had been armed with and emptied them. She went through the guards' pockets and came up with a well-used Makarov pistol. She slung an AK over her shoulder and held the Makarov at her side confidently. "Lead on, Commander," she said. "Let's see what this menagerie has to offer."

"What are we going to find here?" Carter asked Savarin.

The man was beyond coherent speech. His eyes had glazed over and his breathing was rapid and shallow.

Carter pulled out the orange syringe and put Savarin out
for the count.

"Looks like it's just you and me, pal," Jean said.

Carter could see that Jean was scared out of her mind,
which was entirely natural for someone not accustomed
to work in the field. He admired her bravery and would
tell her so after they got out of this.

Carter found an earthen stairway to an underground
cavern. It was narrow and steep, shored up with old
timbers.

"Watch your step," he cautioned her.

While Carter had his attention on the uneven stairs, a
guard appeared at the bottom. A shot filled the small area
with sound. The Makarov barked near his ear and the
guard went down.

"I owe you one," Carter said as he raced for the
bottom.

"Call it even," she said, out of breath.

"No surprises now. We've got two or three other
guards down here and they know they have company,"
he said, crouching behind a crate.

One man came running and Carter got him through the
head with one shot from Wilhelmina. A second shot rang
out and Jean shrieked at his side.

Carter looked around but couldn't see where the shot
came from. He swung heavy crates around them and
pulled the woman near him to examine her wound.

At first he couldn't see it and he'd thought he'd looked
everywhere.

She groaned.

"Where are you hit?" he asked, his tone urgent. They
were still in great danger.

"None of your damned business," she said, wincing.

He turned her over. The slug had creased her along the cheek of her rump. It had shocked her but she'd be all right.

"Brother Schmidt will have included some surgical dressings in the pack." He took the rucksack from his shoulders and produced a sterile dressing complete with antibiotic salve. "Put this on while I look for who shot you."

Carter crawled from behind the crates and searched the lodge from top to bottom without finding anyone.

"Any luck?" Jean asked when he returned, looking a hundred percent better.

"No. Let's look over this place together. They've got to be hiding something here," he suggested.

They began with the cavern, exploring in the dim light of a few naked bulbs. "Look at this," Jean said after they'd been searching for a few minutes.

"Money," Carter said. "A printing press. There's got to be billions of phony dollars in this pile. What the hell for?"

"Maybe to flood the market? Topple the currency standard of the country?" she offered.

"Bizarre but possible. Let's see what the hell they've got here besides funny money."

In one corner of the huge cavern Carter found a mountain of publicity designed to foment separation and revolution. "Come look at this over here," he called to Jean. "Soviet propaganda. Mountains of it. They've already got their propaganda machine at work."

"This will make Cuba and Nicaragua look like child's

play," Jean said, scanning some of the literature. "Come look at this chart on this wall."

"My God!" Carter breathed. "It's a plan to ring the United States with missile bases just hundreds of miles from the border."

"But you'll never be able to show your little find to anyone," a voice from the top of the stairs said. "Good-bye, Commander Carlson, and you, too, Commander Sprague. It was a pleasure."

The figure of Lafontaine's double stood at the top of the stairs. Carter reached for Wilhelmina, but the man suddenly disappeared and a bundle of dynamite sat at the top of the stairs, it's fuse aglow.

Carter pulled Jean behind a pile of printed matter as the blast shook the cavern. They were thrown backward against a mountain of counterfeit money as the lights went out.

They were separated.

Dust was everywhere.

The explosion had buried them alive.

TEN

As the silence enfolded them, all Carter could hear was Jean coughing from the dust that descended everywhere. It was pitch dark.

"What will we do?" Jean asked as she crawled to the sound of his voice.

"We sit and think."

"But we've got to do something."

"We sit and literally let the dust settle," he said, holding her with one arm. They were resting against what had been a pile of phony hundred-dollar bills. "This place is big. We've got enough air for a while."

"But the referendum is just two days away," Jean reminded him.

"It's okay. We've got enough evidence here to kill the referendum."

"It's not going to do us any good if we suffocate."

"Close your eyes and sit back. Let me think for a minute," he said.

"Have you got a lighter?"

"Yes. Why?"

"We can start a fire so we can see. We truly have money to burn."

"A fire would use up all the oxygen. Just let me think for a minute. Sit back and get your night vision. If there's any light in here, let your brain find it."

Carter shut his eyes and let every fiber of his being relax. It was as if the woman wasn't there and he wasn't trapped in an underground tomb. He was back up in the chopper looking at the monitor that outlined the strata of the cave for him.

He remembered the stairs leading to the lower level where they were. The Soviet team had to have drilled some ventilator shafts into the cavern so they could work. But where?

His mind went over the images as the chopper had circled the lodge. Two narrow vents showed on the screen. They were at the far end, the east end.

"There are two vents at the far end of the cavern," he said. "Can you see any better now?"

"Yes. It's amazing. When they gave us night vision training at the academy, I thought it was all bull," she said. "How do you know about the vents?"

"I'll tell you later. Now, let's move it."

He felt his way cautiously past piles of debris to the back of the cavern. A faint cool breeze greeted them when they got to the far wall.

"You were right! We can get out of here!" she said excitedly, grasping his arm.

"Not so fast. These air vents could be too narrow for us to get through."

Jean scrambled up the sloping side of the cavern to

meet the breeze head on. She couldn't get more than her head in the hole.

"Damn! Damn! Damn!" she said, slipping back to the cavern floor, tears streaming down her cheeks.

"Look around for a long pole," he said softly. "We need a long pole and some kind of hooks."

"What the hell good will that do? We're trapped in here!" she cried.

"Just do it, okay? Trust me," Carter said, putting his hands on her shoulders, trying to calm her.

They went their separate ways. Carter could hear her rummaging through the piles of material that was piled up everywhere. He found some metal rods and a role of copper wire.

"Any luck?" he called to her.

"I've got three hooks, but I can't find a pole."

"Never mind. Meet me back at the vent," he called.

When they met at the vent, she looked a mess. Her blond hair was filthy and hung limply to her shoulders. Dirt and tears had streaked her lovely face. Sweat had plastered her blouse to her back. He knew he had to look at least as bad. The black fatigues were sticking to him and the dust was making him sneeze.

"What have you got?" he asked.

"Stevedore hooks. I suppose they used them to shift the bales of paper."

"Perfect," he said, producing the long rods and the copper wire.

"Do you know how to splice these together to make one long rod?" he asked.

"Sure. But what's it all for?"

He pulled the rucksack off his back and showed her the plastique and timers.

"All right! That should do it. Do you always come so well equipped?"

"Used to be a Boy Scout," he told her. "We've got a whiz of a weapons man. He insists I'm prepared at all times."

"When you get back, give him a big hug for me."

She started the awkward job of splicing the rods into one long pole. When she was finished, she ran it up the vent and was able see the tip in the sunlight at the far end. "Do you think anyone's around outside?" she asked.

"I doubt it. They think they've got us out of the way, and the phony Lafontaine's got plenty to do in the next two days."

"Do you think he's the head man?"

"It's hard to say. Probably," he said as he finished work on the last of three timed plastique bombs.

Carter tied a bomb to each of the wooden handles of the three hooks. He set the first bomb to go off in fifteen minutes. With a hook made of double strands of copper, he attached the first bomb and ran the rod up the vent to within a few feet of the top. He set the other two for ten minutes and five, then slid the second up to a point halfway from the top. The third he hooked into the dirt close to the bottom.

"That's it. We've got about three minutes. Let's get as far from the vent as we can."

They lay together, flat against the far wall behind a pile of crates.

"Is this going to work?" Jean asked, shivering in his arms.

"No problem. We've got about a minute before the lowest one goes. Keep your mouth open a little so the pressure doesn't hurt your ears, and relax."

The first explosion rocked the cavern. Earth flew in every direction. When the dust began to settle, Carter moved quickly to see the damage. "Stay here," he ordered.

The plastique had blown a huge hole at the base of the vent as Carter had planned. If he'd planned the operation in reverse, starting at the top, gravity might have been his enemy and plugged them in the cavern permanently.

The next two explosions, five minutes apart, shook the cavern violently. Carter stayed with Jean until the last of the swirls of dust settled. They looked like a couple of moles when it was all over, but the cavern was much brighter. A hole ten feet wide enabled them to crawl to the surface.

"We've got a problem," Carter said when they got to the top.

"What now?" Jean asked, lying in the grass, breathing deeply and still blinking from the light.

"I've got to go down again."

"Why? What for?"

"I saw a pile of heavy steel cable down there. I need it."

"But . . ." was all she got out before he disappeared down the jagged hole.

Within minutes Carter appeared, dragging the cable. "Help me to get this around the haystack over there," he said.

Jean just looked at him as if he were crazy.

"We can't leave the hole uncovered," Carter explained. "I've got an idea. Just help, okay?"

They ran the cable through the huge stack of dried hay until they had it cradled in the heavy cable.

"Wait for me here," he told her, running for the woods.

Jean Sprague stood, stunned, her mouth open, as the sleek black chopper swung out of the woods over her head and settled next to the haystack.

"Will this be able to lift the hay?" she asked.

"According to my resident genius, it won't, but he's always leaving too much of a margin for error."

They hooked up the steel cable and Carter took the ship up a foot at a time. They had to move the hay about a hundred feet.

The small chopper strained, but the huge pile moved. It moved slowly, spilling hay as it was dragged along the ground. With one last effort, it settled into the hole leaving only a slight indentation in the pile as if it had been consumed by a herd of cattle.

Jean applauded Carter's ingenuity.

Carter unhooked the cable and dragged it deep into the woods. When he returned, he slipped into the pilot's seat and patted the floor behind him.

Jean hopped in and strapped herself in. "Let's get out of here," she said.

Near the safe house where Carter had met with Brown, Saunders, and Tanks earlier, the Killmaster found a small stream, peeled off his fatigues, and dived into a pool created by logs that had fallen across a narrows downstream.

Carter swam lazily in the small pond, feeling the grime and sweat float from his body. The cold water was refreshing and cleared his mind for thinking about what he would have to do next.

He heard his name being called from the water's edge and saw Jean. "May I join you?" she asked.

"Be my guest," he responded, swimming a few strokes toward her.

As unselfconsciously as if they were longtime lovers, she took off her clothes and dived into the water, cutting the water with smooth, even, effortless strokes. After a few minutes she turned and swam toward him. Her arm reached out and her hand brushed his shoulder.

Carter held her hand there, forcing her to stand in the chest-deep water. Their nude bodies were inches from each other. Jean stared at the scars on his torso and he watched her pale blue eyes roam over his body. Then she looked up at his face. Suddenly the air was electric with sexual tension. She walked a few steps toward shore, and the water level was soon below her breasts. Water dripped from their tips, her nipples puckered with the cold. She held her arms out to Carter, not saying a word.

He walked to her and she pressed herself to him with a gasp. Carter put his hand on the back of her head and brought his mouth to hers. Jean's tongue was alive, and her fingers pressed into his back. When they broke, Carter ran his lips across her forehead and down her cheeks, licking the rivulets of water that dripped from her blond hair.

Then he picked her up and carried her to the grassy bank surrounding the pond. He placed her gently on the ground, then lowered his body to hers. She embraced him fiercely, the terror of her abduction and escape having transmuted itself into a frantic desire.

"Oh, Nick, I was so scared," she whispered into his hair.

"I know, Jean, I know," he breathed as his mouth sought hers once more.

She pressed her hips against him, then spread her legs so that he could get even closer to her. She savored every second as he eased himself into her. Then she began moving slowly, sensuously, as if she wanted this to last for hours. . . .

The feel of her body under him, surrounding him, was almost more than Carter could take and still maintain control. Her breasts had their own rhythm, sometimes touching his chest, sometimes not. Her legs were now wrapped around his waist, pulling him into her with a commanding urgency.

Finally, he moved his hands under her, taking her thrashing hips in his hands and holding her steady for his final assault. He drove deeper into her until a shrill, half-muted scream tore from her lips as her body moved in one long, continuing shudder. Then the fury of his thrusts brought him to his ultimate destination, and Jean pressed her legs and hands against the small of his back as if she could never get enough.

They lay on the grass for a while, Jean resting her head on Carter's shoulder. Carter dozed off for a few minutes, and when he woke, he decided they should get back to the cabin. They left their filthy clothes at the pond and walked back to the house nude. They found jeans and flannel shirts in a closet and got dressed.

Carter walked into the main room and sat down at the

rustic dining table. He tuned the radio to the AXE channel. "You didn't hear this, okay?" he warned Jean, looking her straight in the eye.

She nodded.

"This is N3. Give me Hawk, Priority One."

The computer-controlled communications system worked instantaneously.

"How's it going, Nick? I've been trying to reach you."

"I've been tied up," he said, explaining everything that had happened to them.

"Keep out of sight. I'll have the C-31 flown to Plattsburg to await your orders."

"Good. I might still need the chopper. I'm going to get my friends together again for a briefing."

"Are you at their safe house?"

"Yes." He gave Hawk a frequency to call.

"If you need anything, call. Day or night."

The statement was superfluous, Carter knew. But he knew it was hell to be sitting at the other end of an operation.

"It might be a good idea to get Carreau and Niles in the picture soon. Time's running out."

"Will do. I've got a few items to handle first." He signed off and called the number Brown had given him.

"Where the hell have you been?" Brown asked.

"A long story," Carter said brusquely. "I want you to get Saunders and Tanks up here again. And keep it a secret. Jean and I are dead as far as anyone knows."

It took them about three hours to appear on the scene. They hadn't all been available, and they'd stopped to buy a few supplies and a large bottle of Chivas.

They shook hands all around, huge smiles of relief on their faces when they saw Jean.

"We thought you were dead for sure," Saunders said.

Carter filled them in on what had happened at the lodge. He told them about Savarin and the phony Lafontaine. "We were lucky to get out," he said at last.

"They're warned now and they'll be doubly dangerous," Tanks grumbled.

"I'm not so sure. I've got the real Lafontaine hidden away. And the phony thinks we're dead."

"Is Carreau still away?" Jean asked.

"He couldn't cancel the western swing," Saunders said. "He's leaving it up to us."

"I've got this feeling that something's very wrong," Carter said. "I believe Lafontaine's merely a figurehead. Savarin was a puppet working for him. Someone bigger is behind this," he went on as if thinking out loud. "What about Boisvert? If the PM is killed, he's the next in line, right?"

Saunders, Tanks, and Brown looked at each other, then turned to Carter.

"Something I should know about?" Carter asked.

"Boisvert's in the hospital. He took a slug in the shoulder and one in the ankle," Brown told him.

"How? When?" Carter demanded. "Don't leave anything out."

"Boisvert was working early at Carreau's desk, and—" Brown began.

"Is that normal?" Carter interrupted.

"No. He's never in until eight or nine. But he was signing correspondence the PM would normally sign."

"But why in Carreau's office?" Carter persisted. "And why earlier than usual?"

"Because the letters were on the PM's desk. And Boisvert had his own work to do as well. He also had to act for the PM during the House session."

"Okay," Carter conceded. "How was it done?"

"Two men in ski masks armed with silenced Uzi automatics. They killed the three SSS men in the hall, then they burst in and unloaded at least two clips each at Boisvert."

"So why isn't he dead?" Carter asked, suspicious.

"The shoulder shot knocked him down and the desk shielded him. One ankle stuck out. He took one slug there," Brown explained.

"Any chance this could have been a setup to make Boisvert look good?" Carter asked.

"Not a chance," Saunders said, shaking his head. "You should have seen the room, particularly the remains of the desk."

"All right. I'll take your word for it," Carter said. "But I want you to give this some thought. Terrorists are not the brightest people in the world. Their leaders might be, but the man with the gun is usually a brick or two short."

"What are you getting at?" Tanks asked.

"Carreau is at his desk early every day. The hit men plan on a specific day. They're comic-book types—these guys don't read the papers or listen to the news. The fact that Carreau was out of town could have escaped them."

"So?" Tanks asked.

"So the hit was set to go and it went. The fact that it was Boisvert was pure accident. He could still have been one of the bad guys and they screwed up," Carter said. "I've seen it before."

"This is wheel-spinning," Saunders objected. "I've known Boisvert since his first election. He's about as clean as they come."

"So squeaky-clean that he sleeps with Carreau's wife to pump her for everything he can get," Jean said.

"Who told you that?" Saunders demanded.

"Everyone knows except Carreau. I'm surprised we haven't heard it on the evening news," Jean said dryly.

"I had no idea it was so public. I'll talk to him," Saunders said.

"Did you bring what you had on the Hungarian exodus?" Carter asked.

Saunders opened a manila envelope and spread a few pieces of paper on the table. They all pulled their chairs closer to get a better look.

Carter picked up a copy of an old snapshot. It was a photo of the family Howard Schmidt had told him about. He looked at it for a long time. "Something about this rings a bell," he said, passing it first to Brown. "Does it mean anything to you?"

"Kid of about ten or eleven and two adults," Brown said slowly, describing the photo as he stared at it. "They all look unhappy. The kid's holding a battered old suitcase and a stuffed animal. The guy's in overalls; his work boots are old-fashioned and worn. The woman's old before her time, her hair in a braid around her head. Typical immigrants."

"Not so typical," Carter contradicted him. "They were trained by the KGB. The couple was subsequently killed by the Soviets because they knew too much. The kid was passed off to another couple, Communist party members, who added to his education. Their deaths were faked and the kid was formally adopted."

"How do you know so much?" Saunders asked, amazed.

"Our people had a defector who dropped this on them years ago. It was covered with the RCMP at the time and nothing came of it."

"So we can trace the adoption back," Saunders said hopefully. "We've got records—"

"Burned in 1960," Carter cut in. "You've got nothing."

"So this kid grew up in this country and could be a power right now?" Brown asked.

"You can bet on it. His adoptive parents were probably two of the best. They would have brought him along expertly. No question that the party supplied all the money they needed. If we didn't know Carreau's background, the kid could be him," Carter concluded.

"Lafontaine's too old," Jean added.

"Not with makeup," Carter reminded her.

"So what have we got?" Saunders asked.

"The Hungarian Revolution was in 1956. The kid was ten or eleven. That would make him somewhere in his mid-forties today," Carter said. "I suggest we concentrate on every man with power in this country, particularly in Ottawa and Québec, who could be or could look like a man of forty-three to forty-six.

"There's something about this picture," Carter mused, again studying the faded photo. "The answer is in this picture. Can you make a copy for me, Fred?"

"You can keep that one. Everything here is a copy."

"What are you going to do?" Brown asked. "You're supposed to be dead, remember?"

"I don't know yet," Carter said. "But have someone send me a makeup kit just in case. I might want to wander around Ottawa. I'd like to get inside the house on Sussex Drive. I'd like to get inside Boisvert's house again. Who knows?"

"Anything else?" Brown asked, his tone showing the respect he was gaining for his new ally.

"A couple of tranquilizer guns, pistols, and several darts. Better get me a camera with special fast film and an ultraviolet light."

"How the hell could you let it happen?"

"He had some kind of special helicopter."

"Where is he now?"

"Buried inside the cavern."

"How much air does he have?"

"Indefinite. We had two vents cut into the cavern."

"Can he possibly get out?"

"No way. I personally exploded the only way out. The whole stairwell caved in."

"Did anyone go back and check on them?"

"Yes. They're still in there."

"All right," the voice of authority said. *"We don't need the material in the cavern until after the referendum. Keep a guard on the place. What about the ones we lost?"*

"Expendable," the phony Lafontaine said.

"Good. Then we have no real change of plan."

"Good luck, sir," Lafontaine said.

"Fool! Luck doesn't have one damned thing to do with

*it. Plan for the future, comrade. I will not always be with
you. Plan for the future and the glory of the state."*

"Yes, comrade. Is there anything else?"

*"No. I don't want to hear from you until we have
brought the Anglos and the rabble to their knees."*

*The line went dead. The man who was posing as
Lafontaine sat for a moment wrapped in thought.* I will
not always be with you, *the leader had said. A cold chill
ran up his spine. It would be impossible to imagine life
without his direction. It had been so long.*

The private line on Thomas Niles's desk rang twice
before he picked it up. "Yes?"

"I'm not at all pleased with the progress. The whole
thing blows in two days."

"I know, Mr. President. Commander Carlson has
dropped out of sight. We're not getting reports from
him."

A silence followed. "All right. I have other ways of
finding out."

A moment later, the phone rang at Hawk's bedside.

ELEVEN

Jean Sprague was a beautiful woman. Carter watched her as she stood by the window of the cabin looking out. Her long blond hair was wet. She had stood under the ice-cold shower until the tank was empty. Her skin was covered with goose bumps. She stood, hipshot, shivering, gripping her elbows to her sides. Suddenly she headed for the bed, then pulled the down quilt over them. "Hold me tight," she said, looking up at him, a question in her expressive blue eyes.

"What happens now?"

"I warm you up and we—"

"I don't mean that," she said, digging a cold elbow into Carter's ribs. "I mean with the Soviet thing . . . with Lafontaine. We can't sit tight here and do nothing."

"I'm not sitting here much longer. When Brown gets back . . ." Suddenly he stopped as something clicked in his brain. He knew it was bound to happen. Something had been nagging at him since he'd seen the photograph. He sat up and turned on the light.

"What is it?" she asked.

"Look at the picture," he said, excited. "See the teddy bear?"

"So?"

"It's old-fashioned, right?"

"Sure. But the picture was—"

"I've seen that teddy bear recently. In Ottawa."

"What? Where?"

Carter's face was one huge grin now. "Our mole made one major error. They all do. He just couldn't let go of the past."

"What in God's name are you talking about?"

"The stuffed animal. Older and a little the worse for wear," Carter said, obviously pleased with himself.

"Will you please tell me exactly what you're talking about or I'll scream? I swear!"

"When I was at Boisvert's house, he had this very stuffed animal on his bed. He's probably been hanging on to it as his last link with the past."

"Boisvert? Are you sure?"

"Sure? Damned right I'm sure. He sleeps with Marie Carreau and we both know he could do better if he wanted a little extracurricular activity. He's deputy PM. Jesus! They all take orders from him. Trouble was, he was Mr. Clean. Everyone looked right past him for the villain."

"So what will you do? Tell Carreau?"

"The PM's already defended him. He's the fair-haired boy."

"Not after sleeping with Marie."

As they talked, a car pulled up in the patch of crushed stone near the front of the cabin. They both grabbed for their clothes and met Brown at the front door. Carter sat his friend down and told him the new development.

"So what's next? We've got to stop the bastard," Brown said.

"Have you had people on him?" Carter asked.

"He's at home, asleep, right now."

"All right. I'm taking the chopper to his place. Did you bring what I asked for?"

"It's in my car."

"Get it. I'm going to get a picture of him in his bed with the stuffed animal, then you can do what you want with him."

Carter changed into his soiled black fatigues, which he'd retrieved along with his shoes before they'd gone to bed, and blackened his face.

"What should I do?" Jean asked.

"You've got to keep out of sight until we've got him and his cronies. A day or two."

He kissed her and headed for the door, when a red light on the radio began flashing.

"Yes?" Carter answered.

"I'm glad I got you. Everyone's pressing for answers. Are you going to make it?" Hawk asked.

Carter filled him in, including his latest intention. "Give it a couple of hours and we've got him with at least twenty-four hours to spare."

"I hope so. The president is really hot about this one."

"Tell him it's in the bag. Even if we don't get Boisvert before the referendum, we've got the evidence in the cavern. That should do it."

Carter signed off and met Brown at the car. He stuck the loaded tranquilizer guns in his belt, examined the ultraviolet-light camera, and headed into the woods to the chopper.

The ride to Boisvert's house took less than fifteen minutes. The area was remote enough that in silent mode, he was able to put the chopper down in a meadow nearby and sneak to the house without detection.

This time he didn't wait and listen for the dogs. He knew what to expect. The first one came at him in a rush, his mouth looking more like that of a jungle cat than a dog.

The dart took effect almost immediately but not before the animal had torn off half his sleeve. It was the same with the second dog. It came at him in one long leap, taking the dart in the mouth but still coming on. Carter caught him by one paw and smashed him against the wall until he was still.

The Killmaster reloaded the two pistols right away. He couldn't assume that Boisvert hadn't detected his first sortie into the grounds and set up a few more surprises.

He was right. A third dog, a Doberman, came at him without warning. It took him by the arm and shook one of the guns free. Carter managed to hold on to the other gun and fire it at an extreme angle.

He missed. The dog had transferred his attention to Carter's throat, but it was open to other forms of attack. As he would have with a man, he kicked the dog in its testicles. While the dog howled and ran in circles, Carter retrieved the pistol and put a dart in the dog's hide.

So much for stealth, Carter thought. There was no way the guards were going to be unaware of his presence after all the racket with the dogs.

With a dart pistol in one hand and a silenced Wilhelmina in the other, Carter moved out of the bushes near the wall as he approached the house.

A guard's silhouette was near the building, partly distorted by a heavy growth of ivy on the stone walls. Carter froze, a dark wraith under a cloudless sky. A gun hand appeared, then a man. Knowing any of Boisvert's men would be KGB and some of the best, Carter didn't hesitate. He took him out with a shot to the head, then finished him off with a 9mm slug in the heart.

It was quiet all around the house. He knew that one other guard would be on the lookout for him, so he froze against a wall and waited.

He waited fifteen minutes. If the man was good, he was doing the same thing. Another ten minutes passed and still Carter waited.

His patience paid off. A large black shape loomed out of the darkness. Carter couldn't see his face. He used the dart gun and the man crashed to the ground like a wounded hippo.

Carter went through his pockets. The guard had no identification, but the Killmaster didn't really expect to find any.

No lights had gone on in the house, but Carter knew that didn't mean anything. Carter crept in as cautiously as if he suspected someone to be waiting. For all he knew, there could be more guards poised to attack.

Carter checked the camera. He had tested it and was familiar with it. He knew he could get a picture in the dark that would have as much detail as a daylight shot.

He snaked up the steps to the master bedroom.

Boisvert was in the bed, but the stuffed animal was nowhere in sight.

Carter put down the camera and searched for the toy. He found it under a robe on a nearby chair and positioned it in a place of honor beside its master's tranquil face.

The shot was not difficult. Carter turned on the black light, then adjusted the camera's focus and aperture setting. He took three shots, close up, at three different settings before he was satisfied.

The rest was no problem. He descended the stairs slowly, keeping his eyes open for other guards.

He had just reached the door and was turning the handle, when two muzzle flashes partly lit the hall. He felt a sharp pain in his head and went down. As he hit the floor he thought of the time. One day to go and he'd blown it. It was his last thought as he felt himself falling into a black void.

Brown stood over him in the cabin. He looked worried. Another black face stood close to him, his attitude more professional.

"How do you feel?" Brown asked.

"How the hell do you think I feel? My head's going to crack open, and I blew the assignment," Carter muttered, bringing a hand to his head.

A hand held a cold compress against his head and he noticed Jean for the first time.

"What day is it?" he asked.

"Still one day before the vote. We should go on the air tonight," Brown said.

The other man put a stethoscope to Carter's chest. "You were lucky, Commander," the man said. "A crease on your left temple and a bullet hole through your left flank. Not bad at all, really."

"We've got to talk alone," Carter told Brown.

Brown nodded to the doctor. Jean stayed.

"Did you take over the lodge and the cavern?" Carter asked.

"The QPP have it roped off. We're bringing the evidence out now."

"So Tim Loomis knows?"

"He's taken over, as you might expect. He's taking all the credit."

"He's welcome to it. What about the camera?"

"Gone."

"That tears it. Is the teddy bear gone too?"

"You guessed it."

"His wife might testify," Carter suggested.

"She and the kids are gone. It's a dead end."

"No way," Carter said, working his brain until the jackhammer inside threatened to burst out. "What about Lafontaine—the phony one, that is."

"I forgot about him. We've got him."

"Good. So the referendum should be voted down, but the mole is on the loose to do what he will," Carter said. "Where is Lafontaine number two?"

"Ottawa. The OPP jail."

"Have him flown here by chopper right now. And ask your doctor friend to stick around."

"Mike Grange? Sure."

"Thanks. So get moving, okay?"

Carter was restless until "Lafontaine" was brought to him. Against Grange's orders and Jean's urging for him to rest, he got out of bed and tested his legs. After some mild yoga exercises, the headache disappeared. "I'm famished," he announced.

Carter, Grange, and Jean were finishing up a huge plate of ham and eggs when the man calling himself Lafontaine was pushed into the room by Brown. He looked older than when Carter had first seen him. All the bravado had leaked out of him. He seemed a shell of the man Carter had met at the Sussex Drive reception.

Carter pulled out his small leather case. "The red one is Pentothol, Doctor. Don't get it mixed up with the green vial or we'll lose our patient," he said for the prisoner's benefit.

"I'm not sure I want to be involved in this," Grange said.

Carter nodded to Brown.

"Mike, this man is either a Soviet spy trained in the Soviet Union or someone they recruited here and trained here. He was going to make the referendum in Québec work, then he was going to do the same out west," Brown explained patiently. "This man might know something about the most dangerous mole this country has ever known. Do you need to know more?"

"Who's the mole?"

"The deputy PM."

"Robert Boisvert? Are you sure?"

"We're sure."

Grange thought about it for a few minutes. His face was grim. "I'll do it," he finally said. "Hold his arm."

Doctor Grange squirted a drop of fluid from the syringe, then injected a few drops into "Lafontaine."

The tall man squirmed as the needle went under his skin. He looked like an old actor, his makeup smudged, hair askew, as if he'd been through the performance of his life. After the shot, he was motionless for a long time. Grange gave him a few more cubic centimeters.

"You work for Robert Boisvert?" Carter asked.

The man didn't answer right away. It was as if he were undergoing some inner battle. "Yes," he finally said.

"Boisvert works for the Komitet Gosudarstvennoy Bezopasnosti?"

Carter had been speaking Russian. He tried the question again in French.

"Yes."

"Where is he now?"

"At home."

"He is not at home," Carter said. "He shot me at his home and took off with his family."

The man seemed genuinely disturbed. Grange gave him a few more cubic centimeters of the drug.

"Where would he go?" Carter asked.

The man didn't answer, but he was restless and fitful as if holding something back.

"Did he have an escape route?" Carter asked, leaning closer to her ear. "Was one of your subs waiting in the St. Lawrence?"

The man struggled with the question for a long time. All his training went against giving out anything incriminating. He looked as if he were going through the tortures of hell. Sweat drenched him. "James Bay," he finally said, his speech garbled.

"Say that again. What bay?" Carter had heard well enough, but he wanted it on the tape that Brown had running close to the man's head.

"James Bay. Power. He has a base . . . a new base of operations."

"Where?"

"At . . . small Inuit town . . . Eskimos all killed off. Town called Nemiscau."

"What's he talking about?" Brown asked.

Carter waved him to silence. "Is it the power supply Québec is selling to America?" he asked.

"Nemiscau . . . going to wire all the dams . . . Boisvert been here long . . . best man we ever had . . . fooled them all."

"But what about Nemiscau?" Carter prodded.

"Last assignment . . . if they . . . find out who he was. Go out . . . a blaze of glory. Blow all the bloody dams."

"He's going to blow all the dams?" Carter asked.

"There now . . . probably started to wire them already."

"Jesus!" Brown said. "The biggest hydroelectric project in the world! Québec's got enough surplus to supply half of the United States."

"And this was going to be his last hurrah," Carter said in disgust. "It wasn't enough to split the country and open it up for Communism, the bastard was going to destroy one of the best natural resources on the continent."

"It's like him," Saunders said. "What a hell of an exit."

Brown reached for the radio.

"Who are you calling?" Carter asked.

"The armed forces. They'll blast the damned base out of existence."

"Let's think this through," Carter said. "If he's got all the dams wired, or even some of them, maybe he can fire them by remote control."

"So a massive raid would do no good," Jean offered. "There's something else we've got to think about."

"What's that?" Brown asked.

"I'd bet half I own that he's got one of their nuclear subs cruising James Bay right now waiting to pick him up."

Carter reached for the radio and coded in his identification to the AXE computer.

"Get me both Hawk and Schmidt on this line right away," he said, then put his hand over the mouthpiece. "You never heard this conversation," he said to the trio with him. They nodded in unison.

"I've got Howard with me. What's going on up there, N3?" Hawk asked impatiently.

"Bear with me, sir. We've got the referendum thing sewn up. You can relay that to the president."

"That was your job. What's so urgent now?"

"The mole—the one you told me about, Howard— turned out to be Robert Boisvert."

"The deputy prime minister? Well, I'll be damned," Hawk said. It wasn't often that he was taken completely by surprise.

"He's skipped, but we have information that he's got one big bang left in him before he leaves us."

"Where is he?" Hawk asked.

"A place called Nemiscau. It's centrally located somewhere in the middle of all the dams the Québecois have built up there," Carter said. "We don't want any big heroics. No big noises. I've got to go in with Howard's Bell 680 as silently as I can."

"Or the bastard will blow all the dams," Hawk finished for him. "What can we do?"

"Two things. Pull all the strings you can and get me satellite shots of the area around Nemiscau. I've got to pinpoint the exact location of his camp. I'll need a refueling tanker on my tail all the way."

"Anything else?" Schmidt asked.

"We think Boisvert may have a rescue sub in James Bay. What you can do is get our Joint Chiefs to coordinate with the Canadian Armed Forces for some choppers, something like P-3C Orion sub chasers to comb the area for a possible escape submarine. Saturate the waters around Charlton Island with sonobuoys. I'd like to see a buoy dropped every hundred yards to be sure we pick up any sonar pings. You'd better tell them to cover the mouth of the Rupert River and blanket it the same way. Tell them to stay clear of the Nemiscau area and not to attack until I'm finished with Boisvert. I don't want Boisvert tipped off."

The silence on the other end lasted only seconds. "I'll have to check this one out. I don't think the president will want to sink a Soviet sub," Hawk said as if to himself.

"Explain the situation to him, sir. Try to get him to see it your way."

"Well, however it goes, good luck, Nick," Hawk said. Carter could hear in his voice that his superior feared for the life of his best agent.

"You're going in alone again?" Jean asked when he cut the connection.

"It's the only way."

"You're crazy, you know that? You're always trying to be the damned hero. Why can't you take a force with you?" she asked, her feelings for Carter obvious.

Brown and Grange tried to look busy and turned away. Grange packed his bag and Brown took him out to the car.

Carter went to her and held her close. "It has to be this way. Anything else could spell disaster." They held each other in silence for a few moments.

"Will I ever see you again?" Jean whispered.

"I've got to go now, Jean. But I'll probably get a few days to myself after this job. Can you take a few days off then?"

"Sure."

"I'll call you. One way or the other, I'll call you."

He kissed her on the forehead, looked into those ice-blue eyes once again, and released her. As he headed for the door his mind was already on the next phase of this crucial assignment. The Soviets in Canada. Too damned close and too dangerous. Boisvert was probably one of the best-kept secrets in the Soviet arsenal and Carter had to get him.

He had to.

TWELVE

Over Waswanipi, a small town according to the grid maps that flipped up on his monitor on command, Carter noted that he was getting low on gas. He called in the tanker.

"Bell 680 calling Wetnurse. You read?"

"Loud and clear. We've got you on radar two hundred miles ahead."

Carter adjusted his radar for a wider scan. He picked up the big ship at the edge of his range. "I'm ready when you are."

The big tanker crept forward on his radar and within a half hour had topped up the chopper's tanks.

"When do you need a refill?" a voice from the native of a southern state asked.

"On the way back. Tomorrow or the next day."

"We'll be relieved before that. We have orders to keep a tanker in the air over this area until further notice," the mellow voice said. "You sure got some clout, man."

"I'll call you from the mouth of the Rupert when I'm leaving."

"Good hunting. Over and out."

When they had gone, he felt alone. The smell of aircraft fuel dissipated in seconds. He settled back for a long last leg.

While the tulips were blooming in Ottawa, a sight that had given him much pleasure, he had long since crossed the snow line. He hadn't planned on this. It would make the satellite scan almost impossible. If and when he found Boisvert's base at Nemiscau, he wasn't dressed for what was to come. He knew he'd have to confront Boisvert face-to-face.

On the Eastmain River, fifty miles north of Nemiscau, Robert Boisvert was leading a dozen long-range snowmobiles on a roundabout route to the living quarters of the men who served the huge dam. Moscow had worked its wonders as usual. Department Five, the Executive Action Department, apart from being responsible for political murders around the world, was divided into nine internal departments, each handling a specific part of the globe. Department One handled Canada and the United States. His control was the general in charge of Department One. Boisvert knew that the Technical Operations Directorate, an unnumbered and highly secret arm of the KGB's far-flung operations, had played a large role in what they called Operation Blackout.

Boisvert held up his right hand and the column followed him behind a snow-covered knoll a few hundred yards from the Quonset hut. Smoke poured from its single chimney. It was probably occupied.

Leading the party, Boisvert unslung his AK-47, the Soviet-made Kalashnikov, a submachine gun that was probably one of the best known in the world. Its banana-shaped orange plastic clip held thirty rounds of 7.62mm steel-jacketed slugs. He held it at the ready as he approached the thick wooden doors.

The men with him were all in fur-lined coats with matching parkas. It was at least ten degrees below freezing, though spring was on the way. The men were Spetsnaz, the deadliest killers in the world. Boisvert was not in their class, but he had received a few weeks of training at their camps while supposedly on vacations in other parts of the world. He could hold his own in hand-to-hand combat with most men.

The Quonset hut was quiet. Boisvert pressed his ear to the door. He heard a Mozart symphony playing faintly. He quickly flung the door open and jumped to one side as three of his men followed, taking cover behind tables.

The three men inside leaped up, surprised. They were hosed down by 7.62 bullets and flung against the walls of the hut, their blood leaving odd patterns on the corrugated metal walls.

Boisvert and his men figured that the rest of the men were at the dam. Moscow had reported a crew of eight.

Boisvert destroyed the radio in the shack, then led his men to the powerhouse, making sure they could not be seen from the windows. With the same deadly precision, they entered the cement building and killed the three men sitting at the huge console of dials. This time they used knives to silence the workers. They had been told not to fire their weapons within the powerhouse. An errant slug could damage a meter dial and warn of trouble. Again, the radio was destroyed.

The remaining two men had to be deep in the bowels of the dam. Boisvert had led his men to two other dam

sites and the situation was the same. The workers were
like sitting ducks. They were not armed. No one expected an attack on remote power dams.

The steep steps to the lower reaches of the dam took
the leader five minutes to negotiate, even in his superb
physical condition. At the lower level, he found the last
two workers. He signaled to the men following him. As
if their job were as simple as mailing a letter, they
dispatched the two unarmed men. They ignored the dead
men, pulling off their packs, each knowing the task he
had to perform.

Within fifteen minutes all the plastique explosive was
set at strategic locations. Outside, two snowmobiles
towed huge sleds of TNT to the base of the damn at the
level of the ice. They were covered with snow and left in
place. The whole dam would be fired when they were
ready. Boisvert's crew had four dams to work on. Each
dam was similar. Each job had been planned down to the
last detail. Time was essential. This one was finished. It
was getting dark. Tomorrow was another day.

At 24 Sussex Drive, all the lights were on. Men
scurried in and out like ants. Television crews were at the
gates but were not permitted in.

Filbert Hume, the head of the SSS, had taken over.
Despite his reputation, this was his prerogative. Hume
was a small man in stature but not in personal esteem, at
least not in his own opinion. He acted like a dictator,
trying to bar Tanks from the house, but was pushed aside
by the massive physique of the chief.

"I want to see her," Tanks demanded.

"This is my jurisdiction. I will not permit—" Hume
started.

"Listen, you little prick. I've never seen you do one damned thing to give you the right to command," the big man fumed, his face beet red. "You're a damned civilian and you keep the hell out of my way." He waved the coroner and his forensics team in behind him and started up the winding stairway at one side of the foyer.

Marie Carreau was lying on her back, a sheet covering her from head to toe. The coroner took the sheet from the top of her head and peeled it back to her knees. He examined her quickly for external wounds, then concentrated on her eyes. Her hands had been placed across the slight bulge of her stomach and her eyes were closed.

The eyes told the story. The medical man carefully rolled her head to one side and waved Tanks over. "One shot through the head just above the spine. An execution. Small-caliber gun. Probably a twenty-two and probably silenced."

"Boisvert." Tanks turned to one of his men. "Get the butler."

When the quaking man appeared, his face pasty as he viewed the body, the coroner quickly replaced the sheet.

"Who was here?" Tanks demanded.

"Just Mr. Boisvert."

"He came often?"

"But she told me it was all right."

"Answer the damned question. Did he come here often?"

"Yes."

"While Mr. Carreau was away?"

"Yes."

"Get the hell out of here."

Brown had managed to gain entrance and was at

Tanks's side. "Take it easy, Walt. We all knew it was going on. We can't play the role of saint now."

"I know. But the bastard! The rotten bastard! He didn't have to do this."

Frank Brown was a compassionate man, but he'd seen this before. "It's never easy , Walt. The guy was a pro. One of the best. Killing her would be like swatting a fly."

"But he had a wife and kids, got married right here in Ottawa. Wife's the daughter of a former senator. I was at the christening of one of the kids."

Frank Brown stood stock-still for a moment like a block of stone.

"What is it?" Tanks said, noting the odd expression on Brown's face.

"You've gone over the Boisvert house?" Brown asked.

"I took Loomis on a quick tour. Then I got this call," the big man said.

"Let's make another tour."

Tanks left the coroner and his men in charge, made sure that Hume restricted his activities to guarding the grounds, and took off for the Boisvert estate.

It was not at all as Carter had seen it on his two nocturnal visits. The gates stood open. The kennels were deserted, as was the rest of the house.

"You take the upper floor and I'll look around down here," Tanks suggested.

In ten minutes they met at the bottom of the stairs, puzzled that they had found nothing.

"Have you called Mrs. Boisvert's family?" Brown asked.

"From the study," Tanks said. He held out his hands, shrugged, and shook his head.

"And they haven't heard from them," Brown concluded. "I don't like this, Walt."

"A guy couldn't just . . . you know."

"I think this one could. Let's check the basement."

It was a two-story house. From the gates it didn't look imposing, but it contained more than ten thousand square feet of living space on each floor, a gray stone Tudor valued at about three million. The furnishings were expensive, all bought from exclusive stores around the world, the walls hung with valuable paintings and tapestries.

The basement stairs were constructed below the back staircase to the second floor. The walls were cement, mostly unfinished. Boisvert had one of the best wine cellars Brown had ever seen. He also had a room-size walk-in freezer of the type used by commercial butchers.

They found them in there. Gretchen Boisvert was laid out on a shelf much as Marie Carreau had been. She was clothed. A similar small-caliber bullet hole was barely visible through her long blond hair.

The children of Robert Boisvert were on the floor at the back of the freezer. Their heads had been bashed in by a blunt instrument. They were in pajamas, as if bludgeoned in their beds.

Tanks stumbled from the room. He sat on an upturned bucket, his massive flanks protruding on either side. He held his head in his hands trying not to bring up his last meal.

"How could a man do that to his own kids?" he croaked.

"He wasn't a man," Brown answered. He was furious. If Boisvert had been close by he'd have been a dead
man, strangled by the CIA's assistant chief of station.
"He was a monster. A monster!" His voice reverberated
from wall to wall in the cool basement until the minor
echoes died and they were alone with their own
thoughts.

Finally, after a long hesitation, Brown moved to the
stairs. "I'm going to tell Carter. He's got to know what
he's up against."

In the cockpit of the Bell 680, Carter had begun to feel
the cold. This crate had not been built for subarctic flight
and neither had he. His teeth almost chattered as he
answered his call sign.

"Bell 680."

"Where are you?" Brown asked. He was still shaken
and he was still angry.

"I'm about halfway across Lake Evans. Won't be long
now," Carter reported. "You weren't supposed to call
me. I was going to report in. What's up?"

"The man's a psycho, Nick. You've got to be very
careful."

"I didn't expect this to be a picnic. What's on your
mind?"

"He killed Marie Carreau before he took off."

"Not unexpected. But I don't suppose she could have
told you much."

"You sound like one cynical bastard," Brown said.
"Is that all you can say?"

"I'm sorry. But it's not unexpected in my game. He
couldn't risk keeping her alive. He might have let

something slip and she could identify him," Carter said, trying to be as sympathetic as he could.

"Okay. Try this on for size. The bastard shot his wife and laid her out in their basement freezer, and the kids were bludgeoned to death while they slept and also put down there."

Carter was silent for a few moments before he responded. "You're right," he said quietly. "A psycho."

Neither man said anything for several seconds, then Carter asked, "You hear anything about my satellite shots?"

"They don't hold out much hope. You might be able to pick up some smoke, trace it back to the shack."

"He's not that stupid."

"Yeah. Insane but sharp."

"Someone had better tell my president. I'd prefer it to be my boss," Carter said. "I can't call him, but I can give you the general code for our computer."

"What do you want me to tell him?"

"Just the facts. Tell him I thought he should know."

"Will do," Brown said into the mike. He sounded sincere and a little frightened. "Be careful, Nick. The guy's a maniac and who the hell knows what kind of organization he might have up there. One guy doesn't blow up a bunch of dams with a few sticks of dynamite."

David Hawk sat back in his chair, his feet on the corner of his badly scarred old desk. The desk had seen many pairs of shoes over the years and as many new pairs of heels. Ginger Bateman had just left for the day but not without leaving a fresh pot of coffee and the usual remonstrations about too many cigars and far too many cups of coffee.

He hadn't eaten all day. His favorite maître d' had not seen him at lunch. He had growled at everyone who dared to cross his threshold. The haze of cigar smoke that circled near the ceiling had rarely been so thick or so foul.

This Canadian thing was going haywire. He'd told the president they'd beaten the referendum threat and the chief executive had been given all the cooperation he needed for the James Bay encounter.

It was Marie Carreau's murder that got to him. It was going to affect the president profoundly. He and the First Lady had been fond of the Canadian prime minister's wife. Hawk knew it was his duty to tell the whole story. That and the carnage that had taken place at the Boisvert home.

It sometimes made him wonder if they could have a mole as close to the top as Boisvert had been in Canada. Hoover had been paranoid about it, as had McCarthy. The Hoover files had been notorious for including everyone in power or who might come to power. He'd even suspected the Kennedy clan.

Finally Hawk cleared his mind of extraneous thoughts and picked up the special telephone he kept in a locked drawer. It was a very private line. The moment he picked it up it rang at the other end.

"Yes?" an alert voice asked.

"I have to talk to him."

"Your code?"

"Donovan."

"Just a minute, Mr. Hawk. He's asleep in his chair. You're sure we have to wake him?"

Hawk didn't answer. The question was rhetorical.

THIRTEEN

Filbert Hume was still in control at the executive mansion, but Saunders was in control of the investigation.

"I haven't been able to muzzle the press, but I've managed to keep the news from the prime minister," he said as he paced his office.

"And how the hell did you manage that?" Tanks asked.

"He flew all the way to Vancouver to mend some fences with the local party leaders there. He was on his way to the Yukon before we learned about Marie."

"And his aides kept the news from him up there."

"I plan to meet his plane tonight and talk to him in the VIP lounge," Saunders said. "How the hell do you tell a man his wife's been murdered? Worse. How do you tell him the man you trained to replace him was an enemy agent, a man who seduced his wife?"

"I don't envy you. Christ! You should have seen Jules's face when I laid the news on him," Tanks said, shaking his head.

"Where is he now?"

"With relatives in Hull. Goddamn shame. Marie was a friend at one time. She was just a down-to-earth kid when I first knew her. She hated all this VIP shit."

"I'm beginning to hate it myself. I've decided this is my last year, Walt. How about you?"

"Yeah. Too many young smart-asses sitting at computers trying to solve crimes without dirtying the soles of their feet. Time for me to get out of it."

The door opened after a sharp knock. An aide stuck his head around the door. "The PM's plane is a half hour out."

Saunders's shoulder slumped as he stopped pacing. "Thanks, Jim. I'll be right with you."

Boisvert sat in the middle of his temporary headquarters acting out the role of a colonel of the Spetsnaz. Eleven men stood around him. The twelfth was at the console of a short-range radar installation.

"We play this one no different from the others. Is everything ready?" Boisvert asked.

"All the snowmobiles are at the front door. The sleighs are loaded," a young officer replied in their native tongue.

"A sighting coming in from the south," the radar man interrupted.

Everyone froze in place. They hadn't seen a living soul that hadn't been designated as a target since their arrival.

"What does it look like?" Boisvert shouted over the quiet.

"Small aircraft. Two hundred knots. It's not on a

direct line for us, so it probably won't spot us. I suggest we let him pass us by."

"To hell with that. He could pick us up on the trail," Boisvert said. "What if it's a heavily armed gunboat? We wouldn't have a chance."

The men poured from the Quonset hut. Two of them shouldered SAM rockets that had been dropped off by a nuclear sub along with most of their equipment.

They could hear the sound of the craft now. The characteristic throb of rotors became distinct.

"A helicopter," Boisvert said. "Blow it out of the sky."

The Bell 680 came in at an angle and was upon them before they expected. It passed to the east while the SAM rocket experts tracked it in their sights.

"What the hell are you waiting for? Fire!" Boisvert screamed.

Two missiles cannoned from the shoulders of the Spetsnaz before they were completely ready. They flew past the 680 so close that Carter was unable to control the airflow around him. The chopper bucked right and left as he fought the controls.

"You missed!" Boisvert accused, facing up to the two professionals, his face mottled red with rage.

"Colonel!" one of the others shouted. "The aircraft crashed. Look!"

They all turned to see a ball of flame in the distance, rising from behind an ice-encrusted knoll. The sound reached them like a clap of thunder.

They raced for their vehicles.

"Stop!" Boisvert commanded. "We don't have time for games. No one could have survived that crash."

Boisvert stood before them, an imposing figure, a man bent on making his last battle count as much as possible. The third dam was on their schedule for today. "Mount up and follow me."

The two men sat alone on two folding chairs in the middle of a deserted hangar. Clearing the VIP lounge would have advertised the presence of the prime minister and the head of the Ontario Provincial Police in conference. This way, Saunders's men kept everyone away.

Carreau sat with his head in his hands. He'd been silent for a full minute. "How did Jules take it?" he asked.

"Hard. I took him to your sister's in Hull."

"Good. She'll comfort him if anyone can."

Saunders sat, one hand on his friend's shoulder, ready if needed but saying as little as possible.

"She wasn't a bad woman, Fred. I left her alone too much."

"I understand."

"I didn't allow myself to get close enough to her in the end. It was natural she'd turn to Robert." Carreau sat with tears streaming down his face. "I knew about it, you know. I let it go on." He sat wrapped in his own thoughts, speaking as though to himself. "I thought he was just ambitious," he went on painfully. "Oh, yes. I knew."

The OPP chief sat, surprised but determined to be a listener.

"I wasn't a good lover. At first I was, but the pressures, the schedule, the responsibilities, you know, it was just too much. I didn't have the energy for her. So I let it go on."

He raised his head and wiped his forehead and eyes dry with a clean white handkerchief. "The only thing that hurt was that everyone knew and thought I was a fool. I didn't think I was a fool: I had more important things to think about. But now . . ."

Saunders had held back on the other murders. Even now he wasn't sure he should tell it all at the same time.

"There's something you haven't been telling me. What is it?" Carreau demanded. "Have you lied to me about Jules?"

"No. It's something else."

"You might as well tell me. How much worse could it be?"

"Boisvert murdered his own wife and children before he left."

Carreau sat on the uncomfortable chair in the huge hangar, alone with this one man. He tried to absorb the enormity of what he had just heard. He'd survived every kind of mud that politics could sling at him. He'd seen his national police force go sour. He'd almost wept when Hume and his SSS let him down. And he'd lost what was left of his drive when Gilles Parisant fought him to split the country.

But this. He'd never experienced anything like this.

"He's been your nemesis from the beginning, Jacques," Saunders said rather formally. "Everything that happened to damage your career was engineered by him. He was sent here as a child for that purpose."

"And it ended with him killing his own family? What kind of a monster could do that?"

"It isn't over," Saunders said quietly.

"Oh, my God! Save me from anything else! What else could the madman do?"

Saunders explained the James Bay threat. "Carlson is on his way up there now. He's requested the U.S. Navy have sub chasers in the waters to cut off Boisvert's retreat."

"You're telling me that this man, this monster, is still at work? He wasn't satisfied to ruin my life, to destroy his family, he's about to destroy the James Bay Project?"

"His farewell gesture. There's never been one like him, and there probably never will be again. Makes Philby seem like a saint by comparison."

Carreau started to laugh, the hysterical laugh of a man who has lost control.

Saunders was about to go to him, to hold him, but Carreau shook his friend off. Typical of his courage over the years, he gained control of himself. "How much does the president know?"

"All of it. He has dealt only with Carlson and the man who runs Carlson. And the secretary of the U.S. Navy, of course, although the secretary knows only the military necessity."

Carreau thought about the great respect the two leaders had for each other. He wondered if the American president would censure him for a fool. But then, he'd had problems of his own. Men like them were targets.

"Get the president on the line for me."

Saunders waved a hand, and an aide ran across the expanse of the hangar with a telephone. Saunders pulled out the antenna and keyed in the numbers for the White House. The Oval Office had been told to expect the call.

Carreau took the phone, a weary man at the end of a battle.

"Jacques. What can I say?" the president said. "My wife sends her deepest sympathies. It's a very bad time for you. We can only imagine how you must feel."

"Thank you. It's good to know you're both thinking of me." Carreau paused for a moment. "They really know how to go after you, don't they?"

"You know the Soviets made you their target," the president reminded him.

"I'll never kid you about McCarthyism again. It's a great temptation now."

"None of us knows who we can trust, really, Jacques. We've got to live with it every day. Now, what can we do to help you?"

"I've been told that you have military hardware in my waters."

"Your aides authorized it, Jacques."

"Give them hell! Just give them hell for me!"

"We'll only be able to harass the sub if we find it."

"Let me try to tell you exactly how I feel at this moment," Carreau said, getting up, the phone pressed to his ear, his lips close to the mouthpiece. "I don't give one good goddamn about diplomacy. Those bastards sat in Moscow and planned all this before I was through law school. They planned to split this country and hurt anyone who got in the way. Now I don't give a shit about one stinking submarine. All I want to hear is that Boisvert is dead and that any Soviet rescue sub is at the bottom of James Bay."

The president had never heard his friend so angry. "The secretary of the Navy will be pleased to hear your sentiments. I'll have one hell of a time explaining this to Congress, but maybe you're right. Moscow has to be taught a lesson."

"Thanks for your support. I don't want to talk anymore. You understand. Give my love to your wife. Give her a hug for me. All of this isn't worth two cents without your woman."

Carreau sat for a long time after Saunders had taken the telephone from him. He wasn't conscious of anyone around him, a man entirely within himself.

Then he shook himself like a dog coming out of the water and stood. "Let's get out of here, Fred. Thanks to that Carlson fellow, we've still got a country to run."

The two missiles had been so close they set up shock waves on either side of the chopper. A more experienced pilot might have righted the craft right away, but it took Carter a few miles.

While he was fighting the controls his mind was at work. He'd stumbled across Boisvert's camp. He'd been too close for the missiles to zero in on him for some reason. If they had been heat-seeking missiles, they hadn't had time to tune him in. If they had been radar-controlled by the operators, he should have been dead. Maybe something spooked them and they fired too soon. Either way, he felt damned lucky.

But now they knew he was there. He thought for a moment and decided on a ruse that he hoped would work. When he had control of the chopper once again, he turned in a wide arc, armed one of his missiles, and fired it into a knoll a few miles from Boisvert's camp.

The explosion was spectacular. A huge ball of flame

and smoke curled into the sky, visible for miles around.

Would they go for it? Would they believe he had crashed? He brought the chopper down not far from the explosion and crept up the knoll, his binoculars around his neck.

It was cold. Carter wasn't prepared for the below-freezing weather in this part of the country and wondered how they controlled the flow of water for hydroelectric power all year. But that was the least of his worries. When he reached the crest of the knoll and focused in on Boisvert's camp, he saw men mounting their snowmobiles.

He was glad he'd brought the M-16 rifle from the chopper. He'd just decided he'd be better fighting them from the chopper, when he noticed they weren't coming his way. In a convoy of about a dozen snowmobiles, some with sleighs attached, they headed away from him. His "crash" had obviously fooled them.

Carter went back to the chopper and brought up a viewing of the locations of all the dams on his console. Boisvert couldn't have been here more than one day. They might have planted explosives at one or two at the most. If they'd blown them, he'd have known about it. He figured they were going to blow them all at once, which gave him time. And it gave the U.S. Navy more time. The gods of war were finally looking on his side with favor. As he walked back to the chopper he felt better, stronger, and more confident than he had in a long time.

His first job was to search Boisvert's camp. The Killmaster took the M-16 from the rack at the back of the 680 and started the long trudge to the Quonset hut. There

was no way he could cover his tracks. No way he could
sneak up on them. Not one tree or bush stood between
him and the deserted building.

As he came closer, the safety off his rifle and the
selector set at three-shot burst, he noted that smoke still
curled from the chimney. It was the smell of a wood
stove and it had not been fed recently.

All the way to the hut he had kept low to the ground.
Now he crawled from window to window around the
corrugated metal building. No one had been left on
guard. He opened the unlocked door and entered
quickly, his M-16 at the ready.

The hut was a complete surprise. Once a trapper's way
station, it had been set up with a dozen Norwegian camp
cots, each immaculately tended as if this were the base
for an elite group. Not one item was out of place. A
corner had been partitioned off for the leader. It was
Spartan, except for the picture of the head of the KGB,
obviously the man's current god. A metal bucket in one
corner contained a soiled square bandage from a wound,
and a long roll of gauze covered with dried blood.
Boisvert's wounds hadn't slowed him down, but the
evidence of his presence was conclusive.

The man from AXE found one thing that was of use to
him. An extra box of cold-weather gear had been opened
and stored in a corner. In minutes he was dressed as
warmly as the enemy. He found a spare Kalashnikov,
loaded it, and tossed the M-16 as far as he could into the
snow.

Out back, a small shed contained spare parts for the
snowmobiles. Two spare machines were gassed and
ready to replace any that broke down. Carter started one

of them and tested it by obliterating his tracks halfway back to the knoll. He retraced his path and started to follow the tracks of the enemy.

Jean Sprague was bored and worried. She was stuck in this damned cabin and he was out there looking for Boisvert. It was so unfair. She didn't know anything beyond what was on the radio news. She didn't even know what Frank Brown was doing. He had promised to keep in touch, but it had been forty-eight hours and he hadn't called.

Frustrated, she flipped on the radio and scanned the dial until she picked up a news broadcast from Ottawa.

"We have no further information on the bizarre killings of Marie Carreau and the three members of the Boisvert family. Yesterday we reported that the deaths of the children had been particularly brutal. We do know that all four were killed by Deputy Prime Minister Robert Boisvert.

"There is no additional news out of Sussex Drive. Prime Minister Carreau is now home, but he will not talk to anyone. Jules Carreau, formerly accused of Gilles Parisant's murder, has been released. His whereabouts are unknown.

"Last in this brief update, voters flocked to the polls in Québec to block the referendum. Reporters on the street have concluded that the revelations that a foreign power was trying to manipulate the referendum brought all the undecided voters out of the closet.

"We will have a full news report at ten tonight."

Jean turned off the radio and just sat, staring out the window. She'd been in G-2 for almost ten years and thought she'd heard almost everything—everything but a foreign agent killing his family to cover his tracks.

She walked to the front door to get some fresh air. When it was open, she leaned against the doorframe, her mind picturing the family of Robert Boisvert.

Jean closed her eyes and whispered to the emptiness of the woods:

"Oh, Nick . . . where are you? I'm so frightened for you!"

FOURTEEN

Nick Carter was seated on the fastest snowmobile that Bombardier of Montreal could produce. It was the commercial model of the machine professional racers souped up for the sport that was sweeping snow country. Without apparent difficulty, he was following the tracks of a dozen other machines.

It was an overcast day but the white blanket covering the landscape was enough to make special snow goggles a must. Through their lenses, everything looked vaguely yellow.

The ride was as bumpy as it was fast. At times the machine took off from a ledge to sail ten to twenty feet through the air to land with most of its weight on the front skis. The back would follow with a bone-jarring thud as the spinning rubber track hit the snow and churned ahead. When he was airborne, the sound of the motor reminded Carter of a boat slipping off a wave and its propeller running free for a few seconds. He had to remind himself that this was a deadly serious business and not a joyride.

Suddenly the tracks of his quarry split up into two groups. Carter followed the group heading to the left and soon saw the massive dam looming up in front of him.

He wasn't prepared for the size of the structure. It seemed to stretch from horizon to horizon, a monolith that made the work of the ancients in Egypt pale into insignificance. It was incredible to conceive that the Québec government had built six this size.

He followed the group that headed for the control building at the top of the dam to the left. He was on a frozen lake with hundreds of millions of gallons under his track. The dam operated all year round, taking in the water from beneath the ice and directing it through its huge tunnels to flow out in a fairyland of ice on the other side.

Carter made a wide sweep of the control tower, coming around at a high point where he could see all the action. Boisvert's men were spread out. Some were in the control house. Others were at the base of the dam on the side where the water flowed from two of the tunnels. One snowmobile stood off by itself, a small sleigh attached.

The Killmaster managed to bring his machine within a couple of hundred yards of the isolated snowmobile without being seen or heard. He walked down the path made by the machine's tracks to the sleigh, keeping his eye on the action around him. He had his coat zipped low enough to grab for Wilhelmina. The AK-47 was slung over his shoulder.

The sleigh was covered with a tarpaulin that was laced down. He slid to his belly out of sight of the others and unlaced part of one side. A rectangular piece of electronic gear sat in the middle of the sleigh, a device Carter had never seen before.

It was definitely a radio transmitter, but very unusual. Why so many terminals and switches? he wondered.

Someone was walking toward him. This was no time for a confrontation. He slid beneath the open tarpaulin, eased out his Luger, and slipped into a slow yoga breathing rhythm.

The footsteps stopped at the other side of the machine. The man bent and unlaced the tarpaulin on part of the other side. A hand slid in and set a frequency on one of the many dials. Suddenly Carter understood: this was a whole series of frequencies that could be controlled at once. But why?

The man's hand was white and soft. The glove he replaced after lacing up the tarpaulin was expensive, definitely not KGB issue. Carter guessed he was looking at the hand of Robert Boisvert.

It took all his willpower to remain where he was. Until he knew how the transmitter box worked, a confrontation could jeopardize the entire James Bay Project. The Soviet crew could have started its work before Boisvert showed up. Most of the dams could already be wired.

While he was considering his action, Boisvert turned and started toward the dam. Carter could hear automatic weapons chattering in the control building. Good men were dying in there, but he could do nothing.

He opened the flap and looked at the huge transmitter again. The casing was secured on the outside by a series of slot screws. He had to have a look inside the console.

Hugo slipped into his palm. Slowly, his fingers stiff

from the cold, he loosened the screws and pulled off one side.

The only thing he could see at his side was a circuit board. At one point all the circuits came together in a short row of minute gold filaments. They crossed over two plastic frame supports at that point. The two supports were only about a sixteenth of an inch apart.

Carter made sure the battery supply was turned off, then drew the razor-sharp point of his stiletto through the filaments. At that point, the break was almost impossible to detect.

His hands were almost totally numb with the cold. He fumbled with the screws, making sure that no scratches were discernible in the plastic around the screw settings. This had to be the master control box. Satisfied, he laced the tarpaulin as he'd found it and retreated to his own machine.

At the crest he'd chosen for his work, he could see a group of men heading into the bowels of the dam. More defenseless Canadians would die down there, but he couldn't act while the whole Soviet crew was spread out. If he failed now, they would scatter or succeed. He wanted to be sure they had no escape route. That would be his next chore.

The day had passed much more quickly than he expected. The only good thing about that was the progress of the enemy. They could only work on one dam at a time. He felt secure now. There was no way they could blow the dams without their master control box, and they'd never find his little job of sabotage.

Carter headed back to Boisvert's base camp. He had to take the chance of another search and he was going to return the snowmobile. The hut was deserted and the fire had gone out. He searched thoroughly for a backup master control box but found none. He was in the clear. He parked the machine he'd borrowed and headed back to the chopper.

Carter started the helicopter and let it warm up. The uneven rhythm of the motor bothered him. There was no way he wanted to be stuck here. He checked his fuel. It was low; he'd have to call up the tanker soon. He just hoped he had enough fuel to do what he had to do.

Slowly, in silent mode, he circled to the west and the huge body of water that was James Bay. When he was thirty miles out, he activated an automatic scanner to pick up the transmissions from the P-3Cs that were working the bay near the mouth of the Rupert River.

When he picked up their chatter, he joined in.

"Bell 680 calling Orions. Commander Carlson heading due west into your space."

"Commander Wright of the frigate *Samuel Morris*," a voice of authority came on. "We have you on our scope, Commander. You came within an ace of a missile up your tail."

"I have you on radar. Estimate I'm ten miles your position. Permission to land."

"If you didn't, we'd be downright insulted," Wright said.

Carter knew the object of the exercise was more to get him in their guns and verify his identification than social.

"We were told to expect you, Commander," the frigate captain added. "We were also told you're not a professional chopper pilot. Do you think you can get down here without sinking us?"

Carter was within sight of the frigate. It was like nothing he'd ever seen before. He'd seen four or five hunting as a pack on exercises, each with its own P-3C, but this one had four chopper pads aft. It also bristled with missiles from every angle.

"What kind of freak boat are you commanding, Commander? I've never seen anything like it."

"Experimental. You think you can get down here without putting this baby on the bottom?"

It wasn't the best landing Carter had ever made, but he survived. The swells were four to five feet ten miles out in the bay. He had to hover for a full minute before he got the hang of it.

In the wardroom, Carter sat with Wright, the two men alone. He had a cup of hot black coffee in front of him laced with an ounce of brandy. He hadn't felt this warm for many hours.

"So what the hell's going on, Commander?" Wright asked.

"Nick would be easier."

"Josh," Wright said, holding out a callused hand. It had strength behind it.

Carter told him the almost unbelievable tale of the men who were dying at the power stations and who was behind it. "I suspect he's got a dozen Spetsnaya Naznacheniya behind him."

"What the hell's that?" Wright asked in his Texas drawl. He was as tall as Carter, bald except for a ribbon of black that he appeared to shave every few days. His eyes were the bluest Carter had ever seen and he had a jaw that looked as if it has been carved from granite.

"Crack Soviet troops. They've got thousands of them

like our Delta Force people. You've heard of them as Spetsnaz."

"Your Russian pronunciation is perfect, Nick. You some kind of spook?"

"Just a good ole boy like you doing the job Uncle Sam gave me."

Wright's brow furrowed. Carter knew the other man had him pegged. He sure as hell wasn't an ace chopper pilot. He glanced at his Rolex. It was time he was leaving. "I need some help," he said, draining his coffee.

"Another cup first?"

"No. I have enough trouble staying airborne as it is."

"What can we do?"

"I need fuel."

"That's automatic. You'll be refueled already. We don't have your brand of hardware, though."

"I've got enough ammunition for what I want to do. How are your people coming with their hunt?"

"We know he's down there. And he's not going away. We've had some soundings, but he's a crafty son of a bitch."

"But you'll get him."

"Absolutely guaranteed," Wright replied. "When are you coming back?"

"Two, maybe three hours if there's still daylight."

"We'll have him by then."

"I think it's time to call in the reserves. What have the Canadians got up here?" Carter asked.

"Couple of chopper squadrons at Kapuskasing."

"How far?"

Wright consulted a chart. "Five hundred miles. Maybe three hours to target."

"Call them and get them up here. Have them check out every one of the dams. The ones still in radio contact will still be manned. The others . . ."

"These Spetsnaz going to blow them?"

"They think so, but I've got them sabotaged. Now I've got to clean them out. If I miss any, tell our friends from Kapuskasing to look for stray snowmobiles heading out."

"Good luck, Nick. When you're finished, come back and see our show."

"Will do. Hey, Josh, a question: What are you doing up here in James Bay anyway?"

"Shakedown. Just lucky, I guess."

"And what is this can you're sailing?"

"Make a bargain with you. It's as classified as hell. But if you tell me who you are and who you really work for, I'll personally show you all the specs."

Carter smiled and picked up his coat and gloves. "I'll be back when you've got your sea monster. Don't run out of those things you're dropping in the water. What is each one worth?"

"The sonobuoys? You don't want to know."

When he was on his way to the camp to see if the Soviets had called it quits for the day, it was almost six in the evening and the sun was starting to get close to the horizon. He'd have to make it quick, whatever he was going to do. And he didn't know what that was yet. When the sun went down at this latitude, it dropped like a stone and the nights were black as a miser's heart. Unless the clouds cleared . . .

Carter widened the scope of his radar and saw the beginning of a cold front coming in front from the west. It was very close. The sky behind it was clear.

Good. All the better to see you by, as the wolf said. And he felt like a wolf right now. The interlude with Commander Wright had not changed the fire that burned in his gut. Boisvert was the worst kind of cold-blooded killer, a robot of a man who executed every order from Moscow as if programmed. The men he led were not much better. They had trained on live men and women from the gulags of Siberia. Their cold steel had not been tested on straw dummies.

It was time they felt the cutting edge of that steel.

FIFTEEN

The Bell 680 Carter was flying was sleek and fast.
Even as an inexperienced chopper pilot, he recognized
its potential. He'd had his hands on chopper controls for
a few hundred hours, but that didn't qualify him for star
status.

All the weaponry was concealed. A bank of toggle
switches at his right hand brought them into play when
needed. In the meantime, his airspeed wasn't slowed by
the multiple racks of Penguin antiship missiles and the
rotary-type cannon.

In less time than he imagined, Boisvert's camp came
at him out of the diminishing light. The cold front had
come and gone. Stars had just started to peek from the
darkening blue.

Carter circled the camp in silent mode. All the time
Spetsnaz were inside. Smoke poured from the chimney.
It was probably dinnertime. He armed himself with the
thought that they would be gloating about shooting down
unarmed hydro workers.

He counted the machines parked outside. They made

it easy for him. In usual Spetsnaya Naznacheniya precision, the machines were lined up in two rows of six with the leader's out in front, the small sleigh still attached.

The circle complete, he moved off for a missile run, wishing he'd had more experience with this kind of weaponry.

He activated all weapons systems and felt the drag on his speed. Then he flipped the front faceplate of his helmet down and adjusted the electronic viewer that showed up as a green set of rings.

The hut was dead center in the rings. The range was five hundred yards. He pressed the triggers on missiles one and six felt the chopper shudder.

"I am proud of you," Boisvert said. The man who had been deputy prime minister of Canada was a colonel in the Spetsnaz. He sat at the head of the makeshift table, a cup of coffee in his hand.

The most senior of his men was a lieutenant. The others were all noncommissioned officers chosen for the job. It was felt that the experience would make them better leaders.

Every man at the table was a dedicated machine, capable of killing in a hundred ways, with weapons or without. They were silent under their commander's praise. They were not expected to respond. Praise was a rare commodity. They cleaned their plates and kept their thoughts to themselves.

The two missiles struck the hut at both ends of the roof and blew out both sides of the building. No one inside moved from the hut as Carter brought the chopper around for a better look. Debris flew in all directions. At first it appeared that he had killed them all in the first run.

Then a few began to stagger outside. They were dazed as they weaved in and out of the machines, each man intent on finding his own. He counted a half dozen. They mounted their snowmobiles and prepared to take off.

Carter banked to the right and lined up the row of machines in his sights. He squeezed the twin triggers of his cannon mounts. They started to rotate, spitting out 60mm shells at the rate of more than three hundred a minute.

Two rows of explosions, each about a foot apart, headed for the snowmobiles. Five of them had pulled away and missed the rain of steel. The other seven were demolished.

Carter took off after one of the escaping soldiers. At first his aim was off, and the shell exploded in front of the machine. He corrected and was too short. Finally, as he corrected again, he saw the gas tank explode on the machine as the soldier fell off and rolled in the snow leaving a trail of red.

He was going to break off and let the incoming Canadian squadrons take care of them, but his blood was up. The Killmaster went after the next machine now hundreds of yards away and ran a string of cannon shells along its path on the first pass.

He hated this kind of fighting. He'd prefer to be up close, facing the enemy, steel against steel, than see them go down as if by remote control, tin soldiers bowled over by a strong wind.

The last of the strays were destroyed and Carter returned to the hut. Men staggered near the gutted building as if they were too shocked by the first blast to try for their machines. The ones that came close to succeeding found their machines to be piles of twisted metal.

Boisvert's machine was missing. Carter scanned the surrounding blue-white landscape for it, but it was nowhere in sight. It was getting dark. The stars were out, but the moon was in the first quarter and no help as a beacon.

He turned away and came back to loose one of the two remaining Penguin missiles. It hit the center of the hut, blowing out the remaining walls. The men who had been standing were nowhere to be seen, either dead or covered with debris or snow.

Boisvert. He was the only one Carter wasn't sure of. Where the hell could he have gone in such a short time? The Killmaster took the chopper in a half-mile circle and didn't see Boisvert's machine. He saw plenty of tracks but couldn't tell which one was Boisvert's.

Carter tried a circle search a mile from the ruined hut, then a mile and a half, but he had no luck.

He decided to start from scratch and returned to the hut. He hovered over the destroyed building for a minute, keeping high enough so as not to disturb the snow, and scanned the surrounding area.

One track led off where Boisvert's machine had been parked. Carter took his craft up to a half mile and traced the track. It led off as far as Carter could see.

Slowly, like a giant bird stalking its prey, he used the machine's silent mode and a slow rate of speed to follow the trail. It led toward the dam he'd visited earlier in the day.

Boisvert's snowmobile was a speck on the horizon ahead, slowly growing in size as Carter gained on it. The sheer face of a cement wall loomed up in front of them. It was time for the showdown.

Carter brought the chopper in close. Boisvert couldn't hear the aircraft for the noise of his own machine. He was being given a rough ride by the ice that had churned upward around the lake as it froze and compressed. The sleigh pulled by the Bombardier machine sped along behind on its flexible umbilical.

Carter brought the chopper around to one side to attract Boisvert's attention. He could barely see the man's eyes through the yellow protection of snow goggles.

The Killmaster circled in front of Boisvert and blocked his path, the multiple pods of cannon facing the Soviet agent. They were empty, but Boisvert had no way of knowing that.

Both men were desperate to win.

Boisvert stopped. He sat for a moment trying to think of something to do. He climbed from his machine, unslung his AK-47, clicked off the safety, turned it to full auto, and aimed at the Plexiglas bubble, all that was between him and his tormentor.

Carter started to react, but the hail of 7.62mm steel-capped slugs was already leaving the muzzle. He lost his grip on the control bar and the chopper bounced on her skids.

The rain of steel hit the plastic faster than Carter could protect himself. The bullets rained against the chopper's bubble at the rate of seven hundred a minute. In less than five seconds Boisvert stood with an empty clip. All thirty rounds had hit the bubble.

Carter put his hands back on the control bar. He was as stunned as Boisvert. Lexan. That was the only answer he could think of. Lexan, the material that looked like Plexiglas which had been developed for the space program. It had been used in many countries to build "popemobiles" after the attempt on John Paul II's life in St. Peter's Square. It was being used in diplomatic limousines. Why wouldn't they use it in a prototype helicopter that had so many other revolutionary features?

Carter started to laugh. By rights he should be dead because he'd been too arrogant. The laugh was more mild hysteria than humor. But nothing was funny in this. He faced a master spy, a merciless, brutal killer, a man who had fooled the world's most astute politicians.

Boisvert had slapped another orange-colored banana clip in the Kalashnikov and was moving off to port where he could get a shot at the motor.

Carter lifted the Bell 680 a foot off the ground and turned to face him. This time as the bullets came at him, he watched them bounce off the Lexan like pebbles off a stone wall.

Boisvert screamed out his frustration and threw the automatic weapon far from him. He ran back to his snowmobile and started to unlace the tarpaulin from the sleigh as fast as he could. His gloves impeded him. He threw them from him in disgust and went at the rope again.

Carter set down on the snow, opened the door of the chopper, and walked across the snow to his enemy. The snow was crisp under his boots. He'd removed his gloves. Wilhelmina was in his right hand.

Boisvert was working on the switches and dials furiously.

"The stupid thing! Made by peasants!" he screamed in Russian, unaware of the gun on him.

He worked furiously, then kicked at the black box in his fury.

"It won't help to curse or kick, Robert Boisvert, or whoever the hell you are. I got to your black box earlier today," Carter said in perfect Russian. "A few small problems with the circuits."

Boisvert didn't turn, although Carter could see every muscle tense. He screamed an oath, kicked again at the box, and on the reverse thrust of his leg, lashed out at Carter with a karate kick, sending the Killmaster's Luger flying.

Boisvert then turned to face him, his face grim. "So you sabotaged the transmitter. So be it. When I have killed you I will rig another method." As he spoke, he drew the commando knife all Spetsnaz carried.

"You're all alone, Boisvert," Carter said, his eyes never leaving the eyes of the killer. "All your men are dead. The United States Navy is taking care of your escape route." He stood leaning slightly forward, feet apart, waiting for an attack. "It's all over for you."

"But now I have your magnificent aircraft," Boisvert said smiling. "Did you think I couldn't fly it? Do you think I have only one escape route?"

Carter maintained eye contact. He could tell better from the man's eyes what he was going to do. The knife was an incidental.

Boisvert rushed but slipped slightly. Carter was able to duck but not before the double-edged knife had slashed through his left sleeve and drawn blood. It dripped from his fingers, spotting the pristine snow where he stood.

"It's just a matter of time, American. Die like a man. No man kills Spetsnaz and lives to brag about it."

"I've killed Spetsnaz before and haven't bragged, and I won't start now," Carter said, his voice calm.

With a wild war cry, Boisvert came at him, feinting to the left but swinging the knife to the right. Again he sliced through Carter's sleeve and the blood came in a steady stream, turning his left hand crimson.

The next charge caught Carter going the wrong way. The knife missed him, but Boisvert's knee caught him in the crotch.

The Killmaster went to his knees in the snow, the pain radiating from his groin. He couldn't see where Boisvert was. Was he behind him? He tried to swivel his head, but the pain jumped up and grabbed him, causing red flashes to explode before his eyes.

The snow had hardened when the cold front came through. Carter's hands were numb with cold. His blood crystallized as it hit the ground. He tried to rise but slipped and slid sideways, ending up on his back.

Boisvert stood at Carter's feet, looking down on him with hatred shining from his eyes. "I'll show you a maneuver we practiced at the gulags, American. It would amuse you, but unfortunately you will be dead," the Soviet-trained mole said as he raised himself up on his toes.

Again he screamed a kind of war cry as he launched himself at Carter. As he flew through the air, the wicked knife in his right hand, he blocked out the last of the light.

At the last second, Carter managed to slide enough to miss the full weight of the madman as he came straight down, parallel to the ground.

The Spetsnaz blade slashed through Carter's jacket, a quarter inch of skin at his flank, and the ice below.

The two men were nose to nose, brown eyes looking into dark blue. Boisvert's face registered surprise. A trickle of blood ran from the side of his mouth. Carter had plunged Hugo's blade through Boisvert's parka into the man's back.

"And that was a new trick for you," Carter said, his voice adopting the tone the other man had used a moment before. "Compliments of all those poor souls you practiced on in the gulags."

He rolled the dead man over, pulled Hugo from its resting place, and cleaned the long blade and the hilt. With pain still pulsing from his groin, he walked slowly to retrieve his Luger. In the cockpit of the chopper he took a moment to apply a pressure bandage to his arm before he revved up the engine.

He took one more look at the body spread-eagled in the snow, then pulled at the control and took off.

It was dark as he headed to the mouth of the Rupert River. He turned the rheostat for the monitors as low as they would go. The cabin glowed a dark green.

Far off in the distance he could see a bright glow. As he came closer, he could see the outline of the sub. The lights were from the frigate. She had the crippled nuclear sub in the beam of a half-dozen halogen lamps.

Nothing moved on the sub. She listed to one side a few degrees.

"Bell 680 calling the *Samuel Morris*."

In a moment a familiar voice hailed him. "Frigate *Samuel Morris*, Nick. We've got the bastard! Blew him out of the water!"

Josh Wright sounded excited and he had every right to be. He was the first skipper of his generation to hunt and kill a Soviet sub.

"We've been waiting for you. You finished up ashore?"

"All finished."

"We've been saving her for you. Their crew is all on board our ship. Got any heavy weapons left?"

"One Penguin and a cluster bomb. I'm not sure they'll make any difference to the sub."

"Why don't we find out, Nick? We'll keep clear."

"Where are your Orions?"

"All tucked in and tied down. The Canadian squadrons are over the mess you left at Boisvert's camp. You're free and clear to take your best shot."

"Over and out," Carter said, taking the 680 a couple of miles to the north out of range of the lights. He had some second thoughts. Shooting at sitting targets wasn't his style. But the president had ordered the sinking as a lesson.

The conning tower of the Soviet sub was in his sights. He pressed the release for his last Penguin just as a gust of wind hit the chopper. His shot was wild. It veered off to the bow of the sub and hit at the waterline.

The huge sub went up as if it had been hit by an atomic bomb. The hull split, and a huge blast of orange and red flame lifted Carter and his craft in an updraft. He lost control for a moment, then brought her around for a second look.

The water was churned up for a half mile around. The *Samuel Morris* was bobbing up and down like a cork, her powerful halogen lights shifting alternately from the heavens to the black water.

"Jesus! What the hell happened? There's no way a Penguin missile could do that!" Commander Wright exclaimed.

"You tell me. You're the sailor."

"She must have had a crack in her hull and you hit it. They carry some conventional warheads. The Penguin set them off."

The great hull of the craft was beginning to settle.

"Take her up about a mile and let your cluster bomb go. Give me ten minutes to get out of the way." The voice of Josh Wright came through loud and clear. "Just let her go. She'll set her own altitude and disburse the cluster. It's probably a hundred-and-thirty-pound CD, so she'll have fifty individual bombs in her."

"How far will they disburse?" Carter asked.

"Maybe you'd better let her go from about half a mile. She'll disburse for about five hundred yards."

Carter took the Bell 680 to a half mile off the broken sub and activated the last of his weapons. He could see the big white bomb coast toward the sub, its nose angled slightly downward. Then she opened and burst, throwing fifty small bombs in a wide circle.

They all exploded on contact. Carter had never seen anything like it. Water churned up to a height of fifty feet in a circle of at least five hundred yards.

Then all was still. Nothing showed on the water that the lights could pick up.

"You got enough gas to make it home?" Wright asked.

"Got a mother hen meeting me, code name Wet-nurse."

"Pleasure doing business with you, Nick. Let's get the hell home."

DON'T MISS THE NEXT NEW NICK CARTER SPY THRILLER

HOLIDAY IN HELL

It was four in the morning, the dead hour, when a normal man's reactions were slowest and his sleep was the deepest.

But Carter hadn't survived for years in the killing business by being a normal man.

The instant the rhythm of sound changed, his eyes popped open and his body tensed.

What was it? A click, and then a slight scrape.

Without moving a muscle, he rolled his eyes to the open glass doors leading to the small balcony. Suddenly a hulk blotted out the moon and Carter moved. He rolled to the floor and then kept rolling toward the hulk.

The click he had heard was the safety of a gun being released. The two dull pops, like champagne corks being softly released from a bottle, were unmistakable. He didn't have to look to know that right now two slugs were embedded in the mattress where, two seconds before, he had been sleeping.

Three feet from the man, Carter came up in a crouch, grabbed the man's right forearm, and slammed the wrist against the doorframe.

There was a grunt of pain and the heavy automatic hit the carpet. At the same time, Carter swung under the arm and twisted it.

His intent was to drive the man down to the floor face-first. It didn't work that way. The hulk was bigger than Carter had first estimated, much bigger, and faster.

With a growl he came out of Carter's grasp and whirled. The Killmaster had no choice. He went on the offensive, dipping and driving his shoulder into the man's groin. He wrapped his hands behind the other man's knee and locked his left wrist in his right hand.

For the second time the surprise was momentarily Carter's. He drove forward, jerking his chin up, tightening his neck and stomach muscles.

But the big man recovered with very fast instincts. The moment Carter hit him, he began clubbing the Killmaster's head with one fist and pummeling his kidneys with the other.

They hit the far wall with a crashing thud and Carter jerked free. He slid to the side, fast, but the hulk moved with incredible swiftness. Carter had a fraction of a second to jerk back and roll his face away so the kick caught him along the neck and under the chin instead of full in the face.

Carter looped his right arm out and caught the man's leg, clutched a handful of cloth, jumped up and into him, holding on and pulling higher. The big man danced for balance on one foot, then swayed aside, and as he began falling, Carter shoved the leg higher and the man fell. As he dropped, Carter slid his hands down the leg and gripped the man's foot in both hands, twisting.

The man grunted as Carter twisted and lashed with his free foot. It felt like a mule's kick on Carter's thigh. He stepped astride the man's leg, twisting with all his power, and doubled the knee, forcing it back upon itself. The man cried out in pain. Carter kept the pressure on, knowing the cry a fake, and the man kicked him again with his free foot.

Carter shot back his right leg as hard as he could and felt the softness give as his heel drove into the man's crotch. This time the agonizing cry was real.

Carter kicked again, once more, felt the foot and ankle in his hands go limp. He dropped the foot and sprang away.

He flipped on the lights and found the silenced automatic, a Mauser 7.63. The gun was a good thirty years old, but it looked new, cared for.

This one, Carter thought, was a pro.

Accompanied by the groans and gasps of the man on the floor, Carter pulled on a pair of pants.

"Roll over, asshole!"

He didn't move. He just lay blubbering and gripping his crotch. Carter drop-kicked him in the side and he went over on his belly, adding new curses to the grunts and groans.

From the small of the man's back Carter took a .380 Llama automatic. He found an eight-inch switchblade pigsticker on his right ankle, and an over-and-under derringer in a Legster holster on his left ankle.

"You're a regular arsenal, aren't you, asshole!"

With one swift yank, the hulk's coat came down to his

forearms, stifling any sudden moves. Deftly, the Killmaster's experienced hands went through the pockets. He removed a flat, thin wallet from the inside jacket pocket, and odds and ends including a set of car keys from the trouser pockets.

"Bruno Copek, from Capetown," Carter read from the driver's license. "Okay, Bruno, what's your story?"

Copek started to roll over. Carter cocked the Mauser and ground the barrel of the silencer into the bone behind the man's left ear.

"No need to move, my man, you're perfect just where you are. Damn, you're a big one, aren't you? I imagine you'd dress out about two-seventy, two-eighty, wouldn't you?"

"Uncock the Mauser," the man growled. "That pin's been filed."

"No shit?" Carter murmured. "Then you'd better start talking before I breathe on it."

No good. The man had guts. Either he was sure Carter wouldn't kill him, or he just didn't care. The Killmaster decided on a new tactic, direct confrontation.

"On second thought, Bruno, roll over."

Taking care, as though he were lying on eggs, Copek rolled over. Grinning like a shark, Carter pointed the Llama right between his eyes.

"Who hired you to off me, Bruno?"

The big man was trembling but he never made a sound.

"I hope you're not Catholic, Bruno. There's no time for a priest."

Carter pulled the trigger.

The gun, of course, was empty. He had released the

magazine and ejected the chambered shell the moment
he found the gun.

Copek grinned. It was more like an evil leer. "The
Mauser's silenced; the Llama isn't. I knew you wouldn't
shoot me with the Llama and make a lot of noise."

"Smart boy, very smart boy," Carter said, "and tough.
Get up, Bruno!"

For a moment, the wildness came back into the man's
eyes. But Carter saw him fight himself for self-control,
move, gathering himself. And then he came up fast at
Carter, not believing Carter would shoot and have the
noise pull the police down on them. He came low and
fast.

Carter anticipated the move and shot his left heel up
with a kick that would have downed a door. The blow
caught Copek full on the upper lip and nose. He went all
rubbery and sighed as he fell.

Carter moved to the bed and ripped the pillowcase into
strips. He tied Copek's hands behind his back, tied his
feet together, pulled the feet up, and tied them to the
hands with a loop around Copek's neck.

He gripped him under the arms and dragged him into
the bathroom. Leaving him crumpled on the cold tile
floor, he flipped the stopper lever and turned on the
water full force. The tub quickly began filling. Carter
rolled the huge body over into the sunken tub, switched
the lever to shower, and let the icy-cold needles wash
across the side of Copek's face and chest.

The big man moaned, moving his head as though
testing himself for a broken neck. His eyes fluttered
open, the wildness exposed again.

Carter sat on the toilet lid and let the cold water drive

all the haze and cobwebs from Copek's mind, and after a few minutes he snapped the water off.

"All right, asshole, let's talk."

Copek shook his head, his tongue probing the gaps where teeth had been. "What you want?"

"Look at it this way, Bruno. Getting shot is one thing. Drowning is another. It's a shitty way to die, Bruno. Your mind screams while your lungs fill up with water. It's a slow death, Bruno. Gimme a whistle if you change your mind." Carter rose from the commode, turned the tap back on to a steady stream, and moved to the door.

"No, damn you, no! What kind of man are you!" the giant sputtered.

"Same as you, Bruno, a heartless son of a bitch."

—From HOLIDAY IN HELL
A New Nick Carter Spy Thriller
From Jove in July 1989